FAILED STATES

Adam Mayle

Orphan House Books

Cover design by Allison Meierding

ISBN - 978-0-9882630-5-5
ISBN - 978-0-9882630-6-2

Published by Orphan House Books

1

They were following him again. Jammu saw their shadows drift across the red dirt road. They were the only shadows for miles. Only a blind man could miss them. Jammu had his problems in this world, but, praise God, blindness was not one of them. In the trembling silhouettes, he discerned the long wings. The bloated round bellies. The scraggly necks. The cruel heads that tapered to razor beaks. There was no doubt about it: the vultures had returned.

Jammu squinted up at the bright sky. The vultures were there alright, lazily cruising on the currents of hot air. Occasionally two birds, half-asleep in their equatorial stupor, would narrowly avert a collision with much wing-beating, screeching, and an explosion of feathers. The vultures were not trying to be discreet. They had no reason to hide. They knew why they were there. Jammu knew why too. It was too hot for pretenses on the African savanna. In a way, Jammu appreciated their directness. If the vultures had not been waiting to sink their beaks into him and his goats, he would have welcomed the company. It was a long walk along the Wanda Road. And Jammu did not walk so well.

Like the attentive herder that he was, Jammu checked on his flock. The thirteen goats were still there, bleating sociably and nibbling the scrub lining the road. The vultures, eager for a chance to pick the flesh from their bones, did not seem to bother them. Neither did the desolate plain that stretched for miles in every direction. The goats marched along, oblivious to a landscape that could be called hellish with only slight exaggeration.

Just looking at the parched savanna made Jammu thirsty. He sipped a little water from the repurposed milk jug that hung from a rope around his shoulder. He swished the water around his mouth, coating his gums with a thin film of liquid. As he savored the moisture, he considered how far he had travelled and how much of the journey remained. Thinking about the miles ahead made his right leg throb. The pain forced Jammu to stop and coax his reluctant limb. Starting with his knee, Jammu massaged his leg, working his way down his calf and shin until he reached the mass of flesh and bone below his right ankle. Jammu was particularly delicate with the clubfoot, which after a childhood of neglect looked less like a foot and more like a gourd that an elephant had stepped on. Only after minutes of kneading knotted muscles and soothing stiff tendons did the pain finally subside. When Jammu resumed his journey, he avoided thinking about the distance still to travel. He didn't want to give his clubfoot any other reasons to complain.

In the extremity's defense though, the Wanda Road would have given even the most conventionally orthopedic foot trouble. The road was one hundred miles of hard-packed dirt that twisted through a harsh plain of dry brush and dwarf trees that constituted some of the most forbidding terrain in the country of Mbanza, if not all of sub-Saharan Africa. There was little to like about the Wanda Road. In a perfect world, Jammu would have taken another route. If he had his druthers, he would have travelled through the green hills to the east. He looked at them longingly. The highlands held the promise of shade, pastures, fragrant flowers, and cool streams – the idyllic sort of setting that thrilled a goatherd's heart. That Eden was a dangerous mirage though, a siren's song. The hills were lovely, but Jammu would have never reached Unubi alive if he climbed them. The rebels controlled the highlands, and the rebels did not like strangers.

Compared to the certain death he would face in the rebel-occupied territory, the Wanda Road was not that bad. Yes, there was no food or water. But even a barren wilderness has its consolations. It was peaceful in a scorched earth sort of way. There was no shade, but there were no trees to obstruct the view. Beyond the vultures overhead – which were getting impatient that Jammu and his flock had not died yet – big beautiful white clouds stretched to the horizon. Not least, the Wanda Road gave him time to think. And Jammu loved to think about Nana.

Jammu had not seen Nana, or been back to Unubi, for a long time. It required some effort to recall the little wooden shacks, the red clay roads, and the green fields of cassava that, despite the best efforts of Unubi's residents, were forever being swallowed by the jungle. To someone as young as Jammu, it seemed like a lifetime ago. All his memories were hazy, diminished with time. All his memories except one: the memory of Nana.

Jammu had loved Nana before he knew the word for the ache in his chest. Since they were small children, when they played together beside the warm, slow waters of the river, he had loved her. While other children played soccer with a tinfoil ball and soldier with stick-guns, he had loved her. Through their childhood, Jammu's love was a thing that he had always hid in his heart, a congenital affection concealed from the world. That was the case, at least, until the day that everything changed.

Two years earlier, the Festival of Yams, Unubi's most important tuber-related holiday, fell upon Jammu's thirteenth birthday. Perhaps it was his burbling teenage hormones. Maybe he was simply carried away by all the yams. But whatever the cause, Jammu's secret love for Nana erupted into the world.

As Jammu trudged along the Wanda Road, he recalled limping through Unubi that day. The whole village was preparing for the festival and filling the streets. The sound of drummers, practicing their instruments, percussed in Jammu's ears as he navigated the crowd. He walked unsteadily, even more than usual. His legs trembled. His knees nearly buckled. His body wanted to flee, but Jammu did not falter. Summoning a courage and determination beyond his years, he stayed the course.

Jammu remembered that he saw Nana sitting outside her family's little house. She was with her mother and her sisters, peeling yams. He caught her eye as she tossed one into the cooking pot. She smiled at him and his heart became soft and starchy like one of the nude tubers simmering at her feet. He desperately wanted to go to Nana, to be near her. But Jammu resisted the impulse. He had not come to see Nana that day.

He tore his eyes away from his beloved and spotted his true target. Nana's father was pushing a yam-laden wheelbarrow up the road to the house. He was surrounded by a group of men, laughing and carrying on as they passed a bottle filled with a cloudy, white liquid between them: they had started into the palm wine. Jammu swallowed down his fears and hoped that the festive mood and homemade booze would put them in a receptive state of mind.

Unfortunately, the expression on the men's faces did not signal an amenable audience. The men, already bleary with day drinking, smirked as the boy with the clubfoot came towards them. Nana's father stopped pushing the wheelbarrow and frowned. Over the years, he had grown to dislike the attentions that Jammu paid to his youngest daughter. They were an unwanted distraction from her chores and the pressing need to find a husband who could pay a respectable bride price. A penniless orphan with a clubfoot would not do.

Jammu recalled standing before Nana's father and the other men. They stared at the boy in silence. Jammu had their attention, but he was unsure how to begin. His heart was in his throat. His thoughts raced. He recalled a queasy rumbling in his stomach as he proceeded to vomit out a string of long-unspoken words that, more or less, constituted a declaration of his undying love for Nana and his desperate wish to marry her.

Looking back, Jammu could not specifically recall what he had said. His emotions at the time were too strong to remember clearly. Regardless of the particular phrasing, his message was not received kindly. The men surrounding Nana's father broke out in laughter.

"Did you hear this boy?" one of the men asked, pausing to emphasize his disbelief and swig the bottle of palm wine. "He wants to marry Nana!"

"Little brother," another man said. "How do you plan on marrying this girl? Aren't you an orphan? You have no parents. No property. You do not even have two good feet!"

A third man clapped Nana's father's back. "What would you think of him marrying your daughter? How about having him for a son?"

Nana's father did not need to answer in words. His eyes said everything. He looked down on Jammu, flushed with rage. Jammu trembled beneath the angry gaze. For a moment, he thought Nana's father might strike him. Instead, he cursed and threw over the wheelbarrow, scattering the yams across the road. Nana's father stomped to his little house, grabbed Nana by the arm, and dragged her inside. That was the last time Jammu had seen his beloved. He left the village that afternoon, escorted by the jeers and laughter of the crowd. Since that day, although Jammu traveled far, hardly an hour passed that he did not think of Nana. As time went by, his love for her only grew, strong and thick, like a yam root. Despite his rejection by the villagers, he swore to himself that he would return to Unubi one day and make Nana his bride. He worked hard to make good on his vow. He suffered, strove, and struggled. And now, after only two years and hardly more than a boy, Jammu had something to show for it. He was a goatherd with a flock of thirteen goats. He had property and prospects. And this new status had not come a moment too soon. News reached Jammu that Nana was promised as a bride to another. She was to be married in one week!

Jammu marched down the Wanda Road, moving as fast as his one good leg could propel him. All his future happiness depended on getting back to Unubi to stop the marriage. But even though the stakes could not have been higher, Jammu could only feel joy when he thought of Nana. With a huge smile across his face, he glanced over his shoulder and admired his flock. He looked into their creepy goat eyes, and it was like Nana met his gaze. To Jammu, the goats and Nana were one and the same. Without his flock, there would be no Nana. They were the key to everything. He counted the goats aloud, as he had done many times during his long journey, puckering his lips as if each number was a kiss for his beloved. The first goat was a kiss on her right hand, and the second was for her left. Goats three and four were for her chubby perfect feet. Goats five and six graced her knees. Goat seven tickled her long neck. Goats eight and nine were for her soft, round cheeks. Goat ten was placed on the belly that would bear their many babies. Goats eleven and twelve signified twin unmentionables. Worked up by the softcore arithmetic, Jammu's lips trembled as he prepared to finish the count. But as he surveyed the flock, he did not see the last goat. The thirteenth goat was gone!

Jammu realized at once which goat was missing. He knew his flock like the back of his dirty hands. It was his smallest goat, a runt of the litter. Jammu looked back down the Wanda Road, but the road was empty, a barren brown strip stretching to the horizon. Shuddering with an awful presentiment, he looked up at the vultures. But their beaks and talons were empty. They did not have the little goat either. Increasingly distraught, Jammu scanned the savanna and tried to remember the last time he had seen the wayward kid.

It was then that Jammu noticed the trucks.

A column of dust advanced along the Wanda Road. The two trucks were the first vehicles Jammu had seen in days. They approached quickly. As they drew closer, Jammu could see that they were camouflaged in dirt and rust. And that their truck beds were filled with men carrying guns. These trucks would bring no good. He herded his goats down into a ditch to clear the road. The sooner the trucks passed, the better. But the trucks did not pass. As they came upon Jammu and the goats, attempting to look inconspicuous beside the road, they started to slow.

Brakes squealed. The trucks stopped, kicking up a cloud of chalky dirt. The noise and the dust drove off the vultures circling overhead. It was as if they too had grave doubts about the situation.

When the air cleared, Jammu got his first good look at the new arrivals. He realized that he had been wrong. The trucks were not transporting men. They were carrying boys – most Jammu's age or even younger. These boys leapt from the truck beds into the road. They wore flips-flops and soccer shorts. If one ignored the AK-47s in their hands, they might have been dressed for a day at the beach. Jammu watched with deep unease as the boys gathered in the road above him.

A slamming truck door broke the silence. A man pushed his way through the boys. The man stood on the edge of the road and looked down into the ditch. Jammu saw at once this man was the leader. He was the only adult in the group. He was also the only one wearing pants and a fancy red beret. A gleaming silver pistol on his hip screamed authority.

"My son," he said, grinning at the goats, "we thank you for your contribution. You support God's work."

It took some effort for Jammu to reply. He had not spoken in days. And his throat was as dry as the dirt beneath his feet.

"Contribution?" Jammu croaked out at last.

"Yes, contribution," the man said. "Fighting a holy war is hard business. Your goats' milk will quench the thirst of our soldiers. Their meat will make them strong."

Jammu looked at his goats. He looked back at the man in the beret. A sick feeling bubbled up in his stomach.

"These are my goats," he said. "They aren't a contribution. I'm taking them to Unubi."

The boys with the AK-47s started to laugh. It was not encouraging laughter.

"Quiet!" the man in the beret barked, scolding them like he would an unruly class. "Nonsense," the man continued to Jammu. "Those are not your goats. Those goats, like all things, belong to God. And we are God's soldiers. God wants us to have those goats, and we'll be taking them."

With this assertion of divine ownership, the boys went into action. They hopped into the ditch and wrangled the goats toward the trucks.

"Those are my goats. I need those goats," Jammu stammered. He was as disturbed by the theft as the sight of others handling his flock.

The boys just ignored him, chattering between themselves as they pulled the goats from the ditch. But the man in the beret motioned for the boys to stop.

"What does one boy need so many goats for?" the man asked condescendingly. He wore a cruel smile and reminded Jammu of a cat taunting a helpless mouse. "Is it fair that some should have so much while others should have so little?"

Jammu considered his answer carefully. He decided on honesty. "I need those goats for Nana," he said at last.

"Who is Nana?" the man asked.

"Nana is the girl I love. I'm returning to my village to marry her and make her my bride."

"A bride? Is this all about some girl?"

"Nana is not just any girl," Jammu said solemnly. "She is the most beautiful girl in the world!"

"Then go marry her," the man said, flicking his wrists as if shooing Jammu away. "Hurry back to your village. We will take the goats off you. They will only slow you down."

"I cannot leave the goats," Jammu protested, still waist deep in the ditch. "They are all I have. If I return with nothing, her family will not let me marry her. They will marry her to Teacher Mapouro instead."

"Who is this Teacher Mapouro?" the man in the beret asked.

"He is the richest man in Unubi," Jammu said. "He has cassava fields. He has goats and cattle. He even has a satellite dish on his roof, which provides many television channels."

"And this rich man. He is very old?"

Jammu nodded emphatically. "He could be her grandfather," he said.

"He is very ugly?"

8

"As ugly as he is rich," Jammu said bitterly. "And he is a drunk with a terrible temper."

The man in the beret shook his head. "That is a shame. I am sure it will be a very unhappy marriage. I wish there is something I could do. But, unfortunately, I need these goats." The man in the beret signaled to the boys. They resumed loading the goats into the pickup trucks.

Jammu watched in disbelief from the ditch, too shocked to move. While he stared stupidly at the heist of his herd, the man in the beret continued to address him.

"I am sorry about these goats. And this Nana person. But, my son, if you want a bride, we can give you brides. We have many, many brides. Join us and you will have many brides too. I will show you the way." The man unholstered his silver revolver and brandished it for illustrative purposes. It gleamed like a diamond in the afternoon sun. "My son, guns – not goats – get women. It is God's way."

Jammu shook his head desperately. "But I don't want women," he said. "I want Nana!" He did not know what he could do, unarmed and against so many. But he had to try something. Jammu scrambled to climb out of the ditch, but he stumbled on his clubfoot. He fell to the ground. The water jug around his shoulder spilled across the red dirt road.

The man looked down on Jammu. He frowned. He saw for the first time Jammu's disfigured foot, which had been concealed in the ditch.

"Then again," the man in the beret said with a sigh, "perhaps it is not God's will that you have guns and brides, my little brother."

Jammu got to his hands and knees. He saw his last goat loaded into the pick-up truck. The boys crowded around him, raising their automatic rifles.

"Now, now," the man in the beret said to the boys. "Lower your guns. We don't need to shoot our poor little brother."

Jammu looked up at the man. The man grinned down. "That would be a waste of good bullets," he said, striking Jammu with the butt of his silver revolver.

Jammu slowly pulled his eyelids open. He was lying in the middle of the road. He lifted his head and saw the pickup trucks driving away. The goats peeked out among the child soldiers sitting in the truck beds. He wanted to scream out after them, but no words came. He could only watch the trucks depart, covering their tracks in a cloud of red dirt.

As the trucks shrank towards the horizon, and the hope in his heart began to wilt, Jammu noticed a shadow on the road. At first, he thought a vulture had returned to claim him as its overdue lunch. But he quickly realized that this shadow belonged to no bird. No bird moved so quickly, or with such purpose. The shadow raced down the Wanda Road after the trucks. An engine buzzing overhead made Jammu look up into the sky. He could just perceive something streak by before the sun blinded him.

While Jammu still squinted, he heard the explosions. The ground trembled. In the distance, the trucks disappeared in a mushroom of fire.

Jammu was transfixed by the billowing smoke. He could not take his eyes off the burning trucks. It was some time before he noticed the crunching sound beside him. With considerable effort, he looked away from the distant carnage and saw a little goat standing at his side. It was the wayward kid, chewing on a piece of scrub brush.

2

No one noticed the eruptive fireball on the horizon. Explosions were a common occurrence in Mbanza. Over the years, the military situation had settled into a routine that was as dependable as the choking heat and cholera outbreaks that plagued the town. In the morning, the rebel Mbanzan Independence Liberation Front – or MILF, as it was acronymized, for better or for worse – would set off a bomb or take potshots at some military convoy. The government would respond in the afternoon by flinging artillery willy-nilly at the countryside.

Meanwhile, the dye refineries belched flames, day and night, making an offering of soot and ash to the gods of extractive industry. So, yes, the residents of Mbanza were habituated to fireworks of all kinds.

The wildlife was similarly unmoved. The lake beside the Hotel Internationale may have been artificial, but the animals were real. Water was a precious commodity on the savanna, attracting fauna from miles around. Crocodiles dozed in the shallows. Antelopes lapped alertly at the shoreline. Elephants, as carefree as fat-calved children, splashed through the lake, rolling in the mud and shooting jets from their trunks. A lone hippopotamus watched from the reeds, its eyeballs bobbing like buoys above the waterline.

The animals were not the only beasts enjoying an afternoon dip. Taking a cue from the local wildlife, guests were making lively in the waters of the hotel pool. Several Russians had been getting progressively drunker and stupider all afternoon. A troika joined by Slavic pride and Johnny Walker Blue belched laughter. The hilarity was raised to a fever pitch when a fourth Russian, wearing only a speedo and the carpet of fur on his back, cannonballed into the deep-end. A huddle of Chinese engineers pushed back their terrace chairs to avoid the chlorinated tsunami. The African waiter was not so lucky. With great dignity, he remained at his post beside the pool, his pants dripping wet, with an auxiliary bottle of scotch at the ready.

If the Russians were analogs for the carefree elephants, Olson was the hippo, sitting at an isolated table, observing from behind his dark sunglasses. He glanced at his watch and flicked his mineral water impatiently. It was too hot to be outside. It was torture even with the patio umbrella. The fake beard didn't help matters either. Scanning the terrace, Olson absently raised the mineral water to his lips. He almost vomited at the first sip. The water was warm brine, an ocean in a glass. Olson wished he could order a beer. A cold beer would have made waiting in the heat with a cilice glued to his chin marginally more bearable. But, unfortunately, a beer wasn't an option. A beer would have been out of character. Of all the things that Muslims could have denied themselves as faith-based prohibitions, Olson was stumped about why they had chosen something as worthwhile as alcohol.

The Hotel Internationale was the only remotely cosmopolitan establishment in the province. Too good for the rest of Mbanza, the hotel sat on an exclusive little hill on the outskirts of town. The green neon marquee on the roof had somehow survived the war, flashing with all the sophistication and glamour that a banana republic could offer. Olson had been waiting at the hotel for an hour. He preferred not to work in such a public setting. It was impossible to control all the variables, to watch all the exits. And a bearded man sitting alone in the scorching afternoon, nursing a glass of warm ocean water, might stand out. At least Olson had the Russians in the pool. Thanks to the drunken horseplay, he was less likely to be noticed – not that there was really much risk of that. No one ever paid attention to Olson. He was absolutely unremarkable. He had a medium build. He was a medium height. His skin was not very light or very dark. If all the races of the world fell in love, mixed their genes, and had a baby, Olson would have been the pan-national love child. He was spectacularly average. He had an uncanny ability to fade into any background, fly under advanced radars, and otherwise disappear completely. It was this characteristic above all others that uniquely qualified him for his profession.

Out of thirst and boredom, Olson reflected on his innate anonymity and began to convince himself that a beer might be a possibility. He scratched his fake beard and looked longing to the waiter by the pool with the scotch and soaked pants. Maybe he could order just one beer? He could drink it quickly. What were the odds that anyone would see? After being stationed in Mbanza for the last two years – *My god, had it been that long,* he muttered – he'd gotten good at hiding his drinking. But before he could act on the impulse, the targets arrived. The beer window slammed shut. It was go-time.

It was not unusual to see Africans at the Hotel Internationale. It boasted a decent steakhouse, a pool, and the largest collection of plinko machines outside the capital. Businessmen from across the province came to hash out deals over Nigerian rum, South African cigars, and float in the laziest "lazy" river this side of the Zambezi. The labor, of course, was all local too. But the two targets stuck out. They shuffled across the hotel terrace in dirty pants and plastic shoes. The short one had the shifty look of a habitual silverware thief. The tall one had an honest face, but a t-shirt proclaiming the Cleveland Browns the champions of Super Bowl XLIX was suspect. Together they stared at the pool and the frolicking Russians as though they'd happened upon the eighth wonder of the world.

It was Olson's job to read people. When he looked at the targets, all he saw was a pair of hicks from the bush. He suspended the judgment though. If half of what Laurent Congolo said was true, these men were not to be underestimated.

The targets made eye contact with Olson and exchanged a wary glance with each other. After visible hesitation, they beelined to Olson and took seats across the table. The Browns fan furled his brow, as if he was thinking seriously or was seriously constipated. The silverware thief, smiling a smile as wide and as yellow as a plantain, addressed Olson in French.

"You are the man they call Ibrahim?" he asked.

In addition to his ability to hide in plain sight, Olson had another notable skill: he was a whiz with languages. He spoke six fluently and could order a drink in a dozen more.

"I am Ibrahim," Olson replied in French, not missing a beat.

The short man's grin became even wider and more insincere. "I am Unrice," he said. "That is Elba," he said, gesturing towards his lanky friend. "We are pleased to meet you."

Olson had heard French spoken all over the world. From Europe, to Montreal, to the Levant. But during his years in the service, he had never heard anyone speak French with such a terrible accent. It was like the man's tongue had been sexually assaulted by a wasp. It took all Olson's willpower not to wince.

13

"Does Elba speak?" Olson asked, hoping to bring the other target into the conversation, if only for the off-chance his French was better than Unrice's.

"Elba? No, he does not speak French as well as I do," Unrice said. "I speak for both of us. I speak very good French." He leaned back in his chair and rested his hands on his stomach with a smug air of entitlement. He looked like a man waiting to be served a Sunday roast.

Olson took a closer look at the satisfied man across the table. Specifically, he looked at his hands. You could learn a lot about a man from his hands. Unrice's hands were cracked and charred. His fingers looked like gnarled tree roots. His cuticles were packed with a thick substrate of dirt. Unrice did not have the hands of a criminal. They were not the fingernails of a terrorist. He had a farmer's hands.

"Were you followed?" Olson asked.

"Followed?" Unrice chuckled. "I was not followed. I know this place too well. I am like a ghost. This is my country." He stretched out his arms with a broad proprietary swoop and leaned forward. "But I ask you, is it safe to talk here? Are there too many people?"

Olson stared at him coolly. "We could go somewhere more private," he offered, lifting an eyebrow suggestively. "Somewhere without witnesses?"

Unrice's smile faded. He turned to Elba and addressed him in their native tongue. It was an obscure African dialect of the click variety. Unrice thought that he was being sly, but Olson spoke it fluently. He had had the misfortune of learning it during his professional exile in Mbanza. Olson had not meant to. He just kind of picked it up, similar to the way a college freshman picked up mono at a keg party. While the conversation between Elba and Unrice sounded like a Geiger counter to the average western ear, Olson understood every word.

"*Do you think it's safe to talk here?*" Unrice asked.

"*I don't know,*" Elba said with a shrug. "*This whole thing is your idea. I still don't know what we're doing here. Is there a reason we shouldn't be safe?*"

14

Unrice considered the question. He turned back to Olson, his shit-eating smile restored. "No, this is a good place that you chose," he said. "Like you, I would choose a place just like this."

Olson rolled his eyes behind his sunglasses. He signaled the waiter for the teapot. Local custom dictated that all business, even illicit business, be transacted over piping hot tea – as if the afternoon wasn't hot enough already. Only after the tea was poured, and the pot was placed in the center of the table, did Olson resume the conversation.

"I've been told that you are from the north. I have some familiarity with the north and its people. But I have never heard the name Unrice before. What tribe are you from?"

"You wouldn't recognize it," Unrice said, cradling the cup in both hands, between slurps of tea. "It's not a family name. My father named me after his favorite food. He loved it very much. It was all I ate as a child. He always brought home bags stamped with it: U.N. Rice."

Olson considered this information and dispensed with the pleasantries. "I am told you and your friend might have connections in the north," he said, getting to the point.

Unrice tilted his head back and laughed. "*Might* have connections? We have many connections. Elba and I have brothers, sisters, and cousins in every village. Oh, yes, we have strong connections."

"I was also told that if I wanted to move certain things in the north – let's just call these things 'supplies' – you could do this. Is that true?" Olson asked.

"You have 'supplies,' eh? Unrice said with a wink. "We can move your supplies. We do it all the time. All kinds of 'supplies.' (He winked again.) We have men. We have trucks. But it will cost you. The north is very difficult. It is a desert. There is no water. The roads are bad. And the people can be very bad too."

"But you can handle bad people?" Olson asked.

"Of course! But everyone must be paid. The tribes. The rebels. Don't even get me started on the police. We can move your supplies. It will not be cheap, but it can be done for the right price. If you know the right people."

"If you know the right people," Olson said, "money will not be a problem."

At the mention of money, Unrice's eyes brightened. He looked like a child on Christmas morning. "That is good. That is very good," he said, hiding his grin behind his teacup. He giggled softly to himself.

"*Why are you laughing? What are you so happy about?*" Elba interrupted in their local language.

"*He says money is no problem,*" Unrice answered giddily.

"*That's good. Money is great,*" Elba said. "*But what does he want for the money?*"

"*What does it matter?*" Unrice said. "*How much should we ask for?*"

"*We don't even know what he wants!*" Elba said.

Olson listened to their conversation with dwindling patience. These were not dangerous men. His first impression had been too kind. They were not hicks. Rather, they were not *just* hicks. Congolo had sent him sheep to the slaughter. What had been a merely miserable day in Mbanza took a depressing new turn.

"My friend asked a good question," Unrice said, returning to his ear-grating French. "We don't know what you need transported? Do you need a big truck? A small truck? Truck size matters."

"We can get into details later," Olson said. "What I need to know now is that you can do the work. That you know the right people."

"We know the right people," Unrice said and poured more tea. "We are great transporters. The best in the north. But you must pay if you want the job done. We need to feed our families. And our families are very large."

Olson nodded, relieved that at least things were progressing quickly. They usually did with amateurs. He removed a wad of bills from his pocket and tossed it onto the table beside the teapot.

16

"What is that?" Unrice asked, eyeballing the cash. He tried and mostly failed to contain his excitement.

"That is one thousand dollars. That is enough to feed a very large family. And it's your money if you promise to do the work. If you swear that you have the connections. That you know the bandits, the rebels, and the terrorists."

Unrice and Elba stared at the money, as if hypnotized. Elba leaned towards Unrice and asked, *"What is that money for? What does he want from us?"*

"A promise," Unrice said.

"A promise to do what?" Elba asked.

"Who cares?" Unrice said. He ended the side conversation and returned to French. "Yes, Ibrahim. We can do this work."

"You have these connections?" Olson asked. "You have done business with these connections before? The bandits, the rebels, and the terrorists?"

"Yes, we know all these people. The rebels and the bandits," Unrice said.

"And the terrorists?" Olson pressed.

"Terrorists? Sure. Them too. All the worst ones."

"You swear you can do this?"

"I swear by the lives of my mother and father," Unrice said. "I have these connections. I have worked with these people."

"What have you transported before?" Olson asked.

"Many things. Big things. Little things. Everything."

"Would you be able to transport food?"

"Oh, yes. We put it in the truck and drive."

"Medical supplies?"

"Bandages, needles, medicine. All the time."

"What about guns?"

"Guns? Why not," Unrice said with a good-natured shrug. "Big guns. Little guns. Rockets. Missiles. We move it all."

Olson stroked his fake beard, relieved that the interview was almost over. "I think we can do business."

He picked up the cash and extended it to Unrice. Unrice grabbed the money, but Olson did not let the wad go.

"Before I give you this money, I need a show of trust," Olson said. "Will you give me a show of trust?"

"Whatever you need. I will give you a big show."

"I need you to do a test run," Olson said.

"No problem. Test runs are our specialty," Unrice said.

"I need you to take this money to deliver a shipment to the north. I need you to swear that it will get there safely. And that you will pay the rebels, the bandits, and the terrorists to make it so."

"I will do this. I'll get your supplies where they need to go. I will pay everyone."

"I didn't catch that. Could you speak up and say that again? Directly into the teapot?" Olson asked.

Unrice thought this was a strange request, but with so much money on the table, he was happy to oblige.

"You are sure you have this power? You have these connections?" Olson repeated.

"Oh yes, I have all the power and all the connections," Unrice said.

"And death to America?" Olson asked.

"Oh, yes. And death to . . . wait, what was that?"

"Never mind," Olson said and released the cash. He had what he needed. He didn't need to push it.

Unrice's filthy farm fingers trembled as they flipped through the bills. He shoved the money into his pants and slapped Elba on the arm to go. Both men stood up and backed away from the table. They started slowly, but their speed increased as they retreated across the terrace. Unrice muttered unconvincingly that Olson would hear back from them very soon.

Olson watched them go. Once the targets disappeared from the terrace into the hotel, he turned his chair towards the street. A few moments later, the two burst onto the hotel driveway, skipping with delight. They were so excited by the money in Unrice's pocket that they practically leapt into the arms of the waiting police squad. Elba, the sensible one of the pair, immediately threw up his hands and fell to his knees. Unrice tried to run, but his stubby legs did not take him far. A rifle butt to the head dropped him like a sack of his eponymous rice.

Efficiency was not a word that Olson often used in Mbanza. Trains were never on time. The electric grid was largely theoretical. Fresh fruit was anything but. But if there was one thing you could count on in a police state, it was the police. In less than 30 seconds, the targets had been disappeared. Their wrists were bound with plastic ties. Their heads were bagged in burlap. They were thrown into the trunk of an unmarked police car, which promptly sped away. When it was all over, Olson felt sick to his stomach. He told himself it was the heat. He got to his feet and went looking for that drink.

When he returned to the table – minus the fake beard, plus one beer – there was a new arrival at his table. It was Laurent Congolo. It was 95 degrees in the shade, as humid as a wet sauna, and Congolo was still wearing a suit. Olson was convinced that the cold-blooded bastard was a reptile.

"Good work today," Congolo said in an affected English that he'd learned in a British school. "Thanks to you, we have apprehended two dangerous terrorists. This operation is a testament to the cooperation between our two countries."

"Yup. Those were a pair of killers alright. A couple of real bin Ladens," Olson said and swigged his beer. "Don't insult my intelligence, Congolo. Do you expect me to believe that those jokers were a threat to anyone? They wouldn't know an IED from a UTI. Where do you even find those poor bastards?"

"What are you suggesting?" Congolo protested with a smile. "We gathered significant intelligence about those 'poor bastards' as you call them. We have damning evidence. They admitted to working with the worst kinds of criminals. Didn't these words come from their own mouths? By the way, is there any tea left? Oh, I'll just help myself."

Congolo reached for the teapot on the table.

"I was sitting right here," Olson said. "I heard what they said. Not that I believe any of it."

"And we heard them too," Congolo said. He removed the teapot lid, inserted his fingers, and picked out a wire. A small recording device dangled from it like a fish on a hook.

"I hope you got it all on tape," Olson said. "Including the part where I waved a wad of cash in their face. With that kind of money at stake, they would have confessed to being Idi Amin."

"Unfortunately, we missed the part about the money," Congolo said. "Your voice did not come through on the recording. You must have been speaking away from the microphone."

"Maybe it was the beard," Olson grumbled.

"Yes, it was probably the beard," Congolo agreed. "Really, why do you care so much? We arrested two men. Does it matter what they did? Whether they are guilty or innocent? These are complicated legal terms. They elude definition. No one knows what they mean. All our superiors need to know is that two dangerous terrorists have been neutralized. That is a good thing for both of us. I help repay the generosity that your country bestows upon my nation. And you get a gold star in your personnel file. It's a win-win, isn't it?"

Olson did not reply. He was in no mood to debate ethics with Congolo. Things were what they were. The less said about it, the better.

"If we're good here, I need to go," Olson said. "I feel the need to take a shower. It's funny how that happens when we're together."

"Yes, I have noticed that you do sweat a lot. It is unfortunate that you have still not adapted to my country's climate. How long have we known each other? Two years?"

"Two years? Who's counting?" Olson said with a bitter grin.

"Yes, time does fly in paradise," Congolo said. "But before you go, I want to confirm that we'll receive the next shipment of – well, *supplies* as you like to call them – tomorrow as planned? All of these sanctions have become quite a nuisance. And now we have these United Nations peacekeepers stomping across the countryside, poking their noses where they don't belong? If not for your great nation, my people would be fighting the rebels with sticks and stones like savages. Which would be a bad thing – both for my country and yours. After all, I doubt the MILF would be as welcoming to the Mountain Dew Corporation as the current regime. Revolutionaries are the worst sort of populists."

"Save the sales pitch," Olson said. "I don't need you to remind me that Mbanza is very important to some very rich people. And don't dare bring up those damn yellow dye # 5 mines again. You'll get your shipment tomorrow at dawn. As long as you turn over the terrorists and keep the dye flowing, you'll keep getting your guns."

"That will be splendid," Congolo said. "Fortunately, we have no shortage of dangerous men in Mbanza. Enemies lurk behind every corner."

"You have my pity" Olson said.

"I don't want your pity. I just want your guns," Congolo said. "But if you're feeling particularly sympathetic, I would also take a tank."

Olson groaned. "I've told you before. I don't have a tank."

"There is no place for lies between friends," Congolo said. "I know you have a tank somewhere, sitting in a secret warehouse, collecting dust. If you're not doing anything with it, why not let us have it?"

"The deal was for guns, Congolo. Light arms. A tank is out of your weight class."

"But the tank would make all the difference in the world," Congolo said, sighing as he considered the possibilities. "The yellow dye # 5 mines would never be threatened again. The MILF would be powerless against it. It would strike fear into their hearts and ground their bones into the dirt. Your country would be happy. Mountain Dew would be happy. And my president would be very happy to add a tank to the nation's fighting forces. He would probably even take a picture on it. Nothing says 'president' like a tank."

"Tell that to Dukakis," Olson said.

"Who is this 'Dukakis'?" Congolo asked. "A great leader?"

"Not exactly," Olson said.

The cellphone buzzed in Olson's pocket. It was fortunate timing – he had as much of Congolo as he could stomach for the day. Olson stood up without paying for his beer. If Mbanza's Provincial Deputy Secretary of "Injustice" was good for anything, it was picking up a tab. Olson muttered a curt goodbye to Congolo and departed across the terrace. The drunk Russians were still splashing drunkenly in the pool. Olson gave the pool a wide berth. He exited the terrace, walked out of the hotel, and climbed into a waiting SUV.

The SUV had impenetrably tinted windows and an industrial strength air conditioner. Olson took a moment to enjoy the respite from the African heat before he turned to the driver, an enormous man with skin burnt perma-pink. The driver wore an eyepatch over his right eye and a soul patch on his chin. His well-worn pants too were covered in patches and resembled a crude quilt. His torso, which was the approximate dimension of an oil drum, was wedged between the seat and the steering wheel

"Beer me," Olson said.

The driver reached into a cooler by his feet, which was filled with beer bottles and lukewarm water that had presumably once been ice. The driver extended a dripping bottle.

"Opener?" Olson asked.

The large man removed the bottlecap with his teeth, which was only marginally less impressive when accounting for the cheap African tin. Olson took the open beer.

"What's the status on the shipment, Kruger?" Olson asked after a long drink. "We need to move it yesterday."

A look of confusion flashed across the driver's face. "Yesterday? How can we move something yesterday today?" He spoke with a thick Afrikaans accent that sounded like a hippo clearing its throat.

"It's a figure of speech," Olson said.

Kruger grunted in reply and let the conversation drop. Olson appreciated Kruger's taciturn nature. This quality was one of the reasons that he kept hiring him. That and he worked cheap.

"The guns are across the border," Kruger said. "They are in the warehouse. But more blue helmets come every day."

"Blue helmets?" Olson asked.

"Yes, blue helmets. Peacekeepers. From the United Nations."

"Peacekeepers, huh? We better get to work then," Olson said.

Kruger nodded. He put the vehicle into gear. The SUV accelerated away, kicking up a cloud of red dirt.

3

Camden expected the fresh air to be, somehow, fresher. After four legs, three connections, and an overnight layover, he had spent the last forty hours in airport lounges and pressurized cabins, breathing recycled air. As he shuffled down the aisle, advancing towards the daylight at the front of the plane, he desperately wanted to disembark and escape the ambient musk of unbrushed teeth, underarm odor, and stale farts. But as Camden stepped off the airplane, the outside world slapped him in the face. The bright sun blinded him. He tried to breathe and gagged. He thought Mombasa was on the coast. But there was no ocean breeze. The humid air was thick and foul like a hothouse of corpse flowers. Baked asphalt and jet fumes goosed his nose. With this sensorial onslaught, he hesitated on the metal staircase that descended to the tarmac. The passengers behind him had no patience after the long flight and quickly started to shove. Camden grasped the handrail and fumbled down the stairs like a blind man.

His eyes only started to adjust after he stumbled onto the runway. His vision clarified and he saw Africa with virgin eyes. As with most things virgin, the experience was a disappointment. He hadn't known what to expect from his first time in Africa, but he had assumed there would be some local color. Something that drove home the fact that he had arrived at a strange and exotic land. A monkey in a tree would have been nice. Maybe a lion or an elephant. Even a gazelle grazing in the distance would have done the trick. But the scenery offered squat.

Without anything quintessential Africana on display, Camden wondered if he could at least see the ocean. According to the map, he was near the beach. But a thick wall of scrubby forest blocked whatever view there might have been. All that Camden could see was the airport. And the airport was no pretty sight. Armed soldiers chain-smoked cigarettes beside fuel trucks. Baggage handlers pushed carts past rotating propeller blades. Meanwhile, passengers of every stripe – mostly Africans, but there were also some vaguely Arabic-looking traders and a few Asians with bulging tote bags – descended like locusts on the luggage, which had been unceremoniously dumped onto the tarmac. Camden surveyed the dirt, disorder, and casual disregard for public safety with unease. It was like he was watching a human tragedy unfold. He thought of the fall of Saigon. The Last Days of Pompeii. Or Bonnaroo. "*Why am I in Africa?*" he asked himself.

Not knowing what else to do, Camden entered the fray to retrieve his bag. As he elbowed his way towards the luggage, he spotted Lukas on the far side of the pile. Camden had only met him in London. He didn't typically fraternize with sword swallowers. Lukas was Jody's friend. The two apparently had met at a circus arts retreat during a study abroad trip in Thailand. It was impossible to miss the Dutchman. At six foot four, with a shaved head and blue eyes, he was the tallest and whitest thing this side of Kilimanjaro. If that distinction was not enough, Lukas was also the only man in sub-Saharan Africa wearing a top hat and a utilikilt. Camden looked for the others. As he scanned the impatient faces clamoring for their bags, he felt like he'd wandered into a minor circle of hell reserved for the sinners of international travel – the stealers of towels, the wearers of fanny packs, etc.

Camden didn't see Piper anywhere. Or Jody. They had sat only a few rows ahead of him on the flight. Of course, their sitting together had not been part of the plan. When Camden booked the tickets, he had placed himself next to Piper and exiled Jody to a bitch seat by the bathroom. But at some point during check-in, this methodically-planned seating assignment had changed. Piper and Jody ended up next to each other in the relative comfort of an exit row. Camden wound up sandwiched between two Chinese men who spent the night coughing and eating cold fried chicken out of a plastic bag.

After much shoving and pushing, Camden spotted his bag. Fueled with countless hours of middle-seat rage, he jerked the suitcase from the pile. For a brief moment, the action, hasty and violent, was liberating. But that feeling was fleeting. The torqueing motion made his stomach gurgle. Something unlodged in his bowels. Since leaving home, Camden had subsisted entirely on black coffee, mixed nuts, and an in-flight fish curry that he had started to regret. In short, he needed a bathroom. Everything else – Piper included – had to wait.

With an awkward gait, Camden followed the passengers heading towards the terminal. After only a few steps, sweat began to soak through his shirt. It might have been winter back home, but February meant something entirely different at this latitude. The sun beat down from above and heat waves rippled off the baking tarmac below, crisping the hair on his knuckles. Moisture pooled in his pants. His thighs tingled with a prickly heat. Again, the question nagged: *what was he doing in Africa?*

Part of the answer had to do with Piper. Camden had never said no to her before, but her suggestion to go to Mombasa for a charitable event would have been solid grounds to start. If she was really interested in helping people, needy people could be found much closer to home. Perfectly serviceable homeless men, unemployed mothers, and drug-addled orphans could be had without flying halfway around the world. Sure, money was not an issue. They had "raised" the airfare through the GoFundMe page – or at least that's what Camden let Piper think. But money wasn't the only thing of value. Time and comfort were a kind of currency too. If they had to go abroad, why did it have to be Africa? He'd heard nice things about Barcelona. Someone must be oppressed in Spain. Piper had never even been to Europe, or anywhere else for that matter. It seemed unnatural for a person to make Africa their first big adventure. It was like a beginning skier skipping the bunny slopes and dive bombing the double-blacks. A year ago, Piper would have been perfectly content with a trip to Barcelona. But a year was a long time ago. Jody hadn't been in the picture then. *"Why am I in Africa?"* he asked. No, Camden was wrong. It wasn't Piper at all. It was all Jody's fault.

With a suitcase in his hand and a bowling ball in his large intestine, Camden stepped gingerly into the terminal. The building was low and long. Dirty windows strained the sun into a dingy haze. Despite the tropical gloom and industrial fans circulating the air, Camden was sweating, just like everyone else judging by the lingering funk. He puckered his nose and concluded that the whole terminal could use a good swipe of deodorant.

While the pressure in his stomach built, Camden searched for a bathroom. He spotted the sign for the men's room: a white silhouette against a black background. His gut rumbled with anticipation. He beelined for the toilet and briefly wondered why the bathroom signage did not feature a black man against a white background, this being Africa and all. But this thought was pushed aside by more pressing matters. Specifically, those matters pressing against his colon.

Camden was already unbuttoning his pants as he waddled into bathroom. It was a small room with one exposed toilet and a long metal trough along the wall. For what Camden had to do, this lack of privacy was far from ideal. But it became even worse when he saw the man with the bun in his hair standing at the trough, leaning back with arms akimbo, urinating in a powerful arch that thundered in the metal basin. Without breaking stream, Jody turned his face towards Camden. A pukka shell necklace with two gold buddhas dangled from his neck. A smile hung on his lips. "Welcome to Africa!" Jody said.

Camden's whole body clenched at the unexpected sight of Jody. His intestines twisted like a noose and all motility ceased. The bowling ball still sagged in his bowels, but it wasn't going anywhere. In a perfect world, Camden could have just backed out of the bathroom. But he didn't want to give Jody the satisfaction of seeing him retreat. Stoically, he unzipped his pants and joined his romantic rival at the trough.

"How was the flight, Cammy?" Jody asked.

Camden frowned. He only let one person call him "Cammy," and her name was not Jody. He suppressed the urge to urinate on his neighbor's foot.

"It was long. It was cramped," Camden said, trying to muster a reluctant stream. "I was stuck between two Chinese men. I think they might have had SARS. Can you catch bird flu from chicken wings?"

"I wouldn't know," Jody said, breezing by the question. "Piper and I didn't have it so bad. We had an exit row to ourselves."

"I bet you had an exit row meal too," Camden said. "It's funny. When I booked the tickets, I didn't remember putting you in an exit row. I'm pretty sure I was supposed to get the exit row meal."

"Is that right?" Jody asked. "The airline must have changed the seats last minute. They do that sometimes."

"I noticed that there was an extra seat in your exit row too," Camden persisted. "If you had all that space, you could have invited me to sit with you and Piper."

"Sorry chief, but the seat was occupado. My bag had to go somewhere. The overhead bin was full, and my devil sticks wouldn't fit under the seat."

With a final squirt, Jody finished. His man-bun gently shook as he jiggled. The absence of his stream pounding on the metal basin revealed that Camden had not started peeing yet.

"Man, it's so erotic here!" Jody said, apropos to nothing, as he walked to the sink.

"You mean in the bathroom?" Camden asked warily.

"No, in Africa. Can't you feel the energy here?" Jody said, rubbing his hands under the tap. "The life. The nature. Everything is just, you know, teeming. I don't have another word for it. It's just so, you know, *erotic*."

"We haven't even left the airport yet," Camden said. "Are you sure you know what 'erotic' means?"

Jody continued, refusing to let Camden's question derail his thought process. "It's a shame if you can't feel it. There is energy in this place. I can feel it on my skin. It's all around us. It's surrounding us, moving through us."

"Jesus, Jody. You sound like Yoda. It's not the force – it's called humidity. And I'd trade it all for a shower a change of underwear."

Jody chuckled and dried his hands. "Change," he mused philosophically. "Change of underwear. Change of seat assignments. Change of life. It's all about change, isn't it? The whole universe is in constant flux. What we had yesterday, we might not have tomorrow. Nothing lasts forever, Cammy. You shouldn't hold on too tight. You have to be like water. You have to fill the glass. It's all about going with the flow."

"And what if there is no flow?" Camden asked, staring at his non-existent stream. "What are we talking about again?"

28

"I'm just talking, dude," Jody said with a smile. He turned from the sink and examined Camden from head to toe, as though he taking an inventory of his soul.

Jody's gaze made Camden deeply uncomfortable. His inability to do something as basic and biological as peeing became an intolerable and shameful thing.

"I think I'm dehydrated," Camden said. He knit his brow and clenched his prostate, desperate to urinate. He flexed every muscle from his taint to his tip, but his bladder did not muster a drop. But while no urine came, something else arose. His straining awoke his dormant bowels, which trembled and unleashed an eruption. What sounded like a chorus of ducks, quacking as one, echoed through the bathroom.

"I don't feel well," Camden muttered after the fact. "I'm dehydrated," he said bashfully.

Jody quickly finished with the paper towel and fled the fouled space, leaving Camden to his shame.

After a respectable amount of time had passed, Camden emerged from the bathroom. Despite the chaos of travelers in the terminal, it was not hard to find his companions. As the only white people in the line for customs, they stood out like dandruff on a dark collar. He saw Lukas first, a head taller than anyone else and wearing his top hat. The two Bulgarian mimes were there too. They were also circus friends of Jody's. They were dressed like a pair of Slavic Stevie Nickses. They might have been pretty if they had not been translucently thin. Since meeting up with them in Addis, Camden had only seen them eat their cuticles. Like Lukas the sword-swallowing Dutchman, they were new acquaintances. The only thing Camden knew about them, aside from their country of origin, was their commitment to miming. They hadn't said a word to him since they met. He had no idea whether they were sisters, lovers, or just creepy friends with telepathic powers. Ultimately, this was not a mystery he cared to solve. He had his hands full with Piper, and she was confounding enough.

Piper stood at the back of the group, wearing a loose blouse and elephant pants. She was a skinny girl with ginger red hair, freckles, and the complexion of a dryer sheet. Based solely on melatonin, she was probably the person least suited for the equatorial African climate. Despite this propensity for sunburns, she was having a fine time. Unfortunately, it was with Jody.

Jody and Piper were playing "Slap Hands," which, as the name suggests, involves taking turns slapping the back of each other's hands. Piper had her arms outstretched with palms faced down. Jody held his hands under hers, tickling her palms with his fingers and delivering swift taps before she could pull away. His every touch was like an electric spark that stimulated Piper's giggle response and caused her to hop from side to side. Piper was losing and loving it. Camden couldn't bear to watch. He pushed through a group of robed Africans, determined to put an end to the hanky-panky. As he approached, he started to sing in the key of Toto. "It's going take a lot to drag me away from you. There's nothing that a hundred men or more could ever do!" he sang, bellowing the first chorus of *Africa*.

Camden achieved his goal of interrupting the game, but immediately regretted his song choice. The lyrics struck uncomfortably close to home. Instead of a cheerful rendition of a benignly-racist ballad, his words came across as a deranged oath from a spurned lover, which wasn't far from the truth. His serenade annoyed Jody, which Camden would have considered a victory all things being equal. But Piper's reaction was gutting. Her big green eyes filled with sadness and her head tilted to the side as though pity were too much for her delicate neck to bear.

"I bless the rains down in Africa?" Camden concluded sheepishly. "What? No Toto fans?"

Neither Piper nor Jody replied. The customs line inched forward.

Given the circumstances, three made awkward company. Jody decided to chat up Lukas and the twins. Piper and Camden remained together. A cloud hung over them.

"Are you feeling okay, Cammy?" Piper asked once they were alone.

"What do you mean?" Camden asked.

"You're acting funny. Do you feel sick? Jody was worried that you might be a little, umm, dehydrated."

"Really? That's very considerate of him," Camden said curtly.

"Well, that's the way Jody is. He cares about people."

"I bet he does. But I'm fine. Despite what Jody said, I am not dehydrated. I have the perfect amount of liquid in my body."

"Don't be that way, Cammy," Piper said. "If you don't feel well, it's fine to say so. It's natural to feel off after a flight. It's impossible to fly halfway around the world and stay in balance. At least that's what Jody says, and he's been everywhere. Did you know that he was conceived at Woodstock?"

"You mean *the* Woodstock?" Camden asked. "Wouldn't that make him like," he struggled with the math, "fifty or something?" "No, not *the* Woodstock," Piper said. "The one in 1997. But it's still really cool."

"Piper, it's not cool. That was the Woodstock with Kid Rock."

"Well, I think it's neat. And my point is that Jody has been around the block. You should listen to him. Like he says, you have to be like a glass of water – you know, go with the flow."

"I feel a little uncomfortable where this conversation is flowing right now," Camden said.

Piper pouted playfully. Her rosy cheeks were unclouded by complicated thoughts. "Cammy, you know that we only want the best for you. We're all friends, right? This is a safe space."

"If this is a safe space, why are there so many soldiers? Camden asked, nodding towards a group of uniformed men with machine guns. "I don't know why we had to travel all the way to Africa for spring break."

"Of course, you do, silly," Piper said. "We're here to do something different. Something special. We're here to help people. We're going to be a part of something bigger than ourselves."

"I know, I know. It's really important to help people," he said, struggling to sound as if he cared. "But why does it have to be such a big production? With that Dutch giant? And those Bulgarian mimes? Don't you ever miss when we were a two-person act? It was just you, me, and a dozen juggling balls?"

"Those times were, well, nice," Piper said diplomatically. "But there is more to life than juggling. Thanks to Jody, I know that now. There are also cartwheels and handstands."

"I just miss the juggling sometimes," Camden sulked.

"Oh, Cammy. Don't be that way," she said and took him by the hand. Camden let her hold it. He knew this was pity, that he was neck-deep in the friend zone, but he took what he could get. If it was up to him, Piper could have held his hand forever. But, sadly, forever was not in the offing.

"Hey, hey, hey. Why the long face, Cammy?" Jody said, reappearing behind Piper. He grabbed her by the forearms and rested his chin on her shoulder. "Still dehydrated, buddy?"

"Jody, stop," Piper giggled as his fingers, freshly henna'd for the trip, massaged her arms. "Cammy's not feeling well. Come on, ooh, stop!"

"Yes, Jody, please stop," Camden said with tone of a birthday boy whose cake had fallen on the floor.

"Oh, he knows I'm teasing," Jody said. "It's no big deal. Every time I do some serious traveling, I catch something. Tulum. Costa Rica. Thailand. It just goes with the territory. It happens to everyone. You just need to relax and get past it. There is no time for embarrassment. During the next two weeks, we're going to spend a lot of time together. Learn a lot about each other. We need to depend on each other and be completely open. It might be a little scary. We're going to be close. Some people might say it's too close. But I think it's never close enough."

Halfway through his speech, Jody had stopped pretending that his words were in any way meant for Camden. His attentions were focused like a laser on Piper. He whispered into her ear and his fingers kneaded her arms like cookie dough.

Piper nodded along as though Jody expressed coherent ideas. But Jody's words made Camden's head hurt. He wondered if bullshit could cause an aneurysm. His face twisted like he was having a minor stroke, which distracted Piper from her massage.

"Is something wrong?" she asked. "You look like you're in pain."

"Is it dehydration?" Jody asked.

"I'm fine," Camden said unconvincingly. "I just want to get to the hotel."

"I hear that," Piper said, accepting the explanation. "We could all use a shower and a nap. Especially you, Jody. Did you get any sleep on the flight? I used you as a pillow all night."

"My neck's a little stiff, but I'll survive," he said gallantly.

"My neck hurts too. I'm so tight," she said, shrugging her shoulders.

Jody took Piper's complaint as an invitation to spiderwalk his fingers up the back of her arms and start massaging her neck.

As he molded her flesh, she threw her head back and gasped. "Jody, your hands are magic!" Mid-moan, her eyes narrowed and flickered like a dull penny. She had had a thought.

"Once we get settled at the hotel, wouldn't it be great to get everyone together and do some yoga? Maybe some group massage?"

"Are we talking cuddle puddles?" Jody asked.

"I wouldn't rule anything out," she said. "Not after that flight."

"I agree," Jody said. "A little massage would do a world of good. And after we get back in touch with our bodies, maybe we can do some base work too. We need to get our acro on before the festival."

"That's a great idea! We need to rehearse if we're going to put on the best show! What would we do without you, Jody? You're the best base around," Piper said, beating her eyelashes with only slightly exaggerated adoration.

At that moment, Camden wished he could have been anywhere else in the world. He wondered how far he would get if he pushed through the line and ran past the customs desk. Judging by the gun-toting soldiers, it would not be far. But there were worse things than dying in a hail of bullets. Watching the woman he loved plan an erotic massage with a man he hated was proof of that.

The line moved forward. The only obstacle now standing between Camden and freedom was a Chinese man arguing with a customs agent over an open suitcase. It was a fruitless exchange. The Chinese traveler didn't speak French. The customs agent didn't speak Chinese. Both sides barked at each other like language comprehension was a function of volume. While the line waited, a busker with a bongo posted beside the customs line. Jody, in addition to being an acro yoga master and a practitioner of the dark arts of devil sticks, was also an avid hand drummer. He was drawn to the bongo like a moth to a flame. Camden was relieved to have Piper to himself again, if only for a moment.

Piper frowned at her cell phone. "Do you have directions to the hotel? I can't get a signal."

"My phone's dead," Camden said. He had drained the battery blasting music all night to block out the sound of his seatmates picking cold fried chicken from a plastic bag.

"I don't think there is any WIFI," Piper said. "Have you ever heard of an airport without WIFI?"

"No, but we'll be okay," Camden said. "I have the hotel's address in my bag. I printed out a map just in case."

"Wow. Like a *paper* map?" Piper said. "This really is an adventure!" She bestowed on Camden a gummy smile. "We're really off the grid. It's like we're going to go search for a lot city of gold or something. Don't you just feel like an old-timey explorer? *Dr. Livingstone, I presume*?" she hammed in an atrocious British accent. "Oh, don't look at me that way, Cammy. How many people go to Africa on their spring break?"

"No one else that I know," Camden said.

"I can't believe this is really happening. That we even raised the money through crowdfunding. I mean, $10,000! This has to be fate. Our plan is resonating with the universe. How many people donated to the campaign again? I'm terrible with numbers."

"Lots," Camden said brusquely. The trip's funding was a sensitive subject.

"How many are 'lots'?"

"I don't know. 10,000?" he said, reluctant to get into specifics.

"Everyone gave a dollar?" Piper asked.

"Some a little more. Some a little less."

Piper nodded as she considered the figure. "It's just like the commercials about helping people for a dollar a day. I feel like Sally Struthers. But we're not giving them coffee. We give smiles. I think this might be the most important thing that I'll ever do. Cammy, you know what? You made this happen. This would have never happened without you."

"That's an understatement," Camden muttered, cringing at the extra ten-thousand dollars he'd taken out in student loans to pay for the trip.

"Understatement?" Piper asked. "What do you mean?"

"I just was just saying that you're *overstating* it," he said, recovering. "The donors that contributed. They're the ones that made this happen."

Piper smiled. "That's so kind of you. Always thinking of others. You really are such a nice guy, you know that?"

Camden did know that. He was a nice guy. He hadn't wanted to go to Africa. He certainly didn't like paying for it. Lesser men might have gloated over the contribution. They might hold it over Piper's head for advantage. That sort of thing was beneath Camden. He might have been exiled to the friend-zone, but he had his dignity. He was nothing like Jody, who was off beating some busker's bongo. Hand drummers were not nice guys. They were not boyfriend material. They were heartbreakers. Piper would find that out eventually. Camden was sure

35

of it. And when she did, once her heart was shattered, he would be there, waiting to help her pick up the pieces.

The bottleneck at the customs desk broke. The Chinese man stomped away with his luggage. The customs agent waved Camden forward with a weary gesture. He took Camden's passport without a word and flipped listlessly through the pages. He looked exhausted. Camden couldn't blame him. Given the heat, the humidity, and the human funk, it seemed natural to go about one's job in a stupor. The customs agent gestured for Camden's suitcase. Camden lifted it onto the desk and opened it. For the first time during their interview, the agent's eyes opened wide.

Camden was not surprised by the reaction. He was expecting it. On top of his toiletries, neatly folded clothes, a veritable pharmacy of anti-diarrheals, anti-malarials, and anti-microbial soap sat an assortment of juggling balls and a pair of enormous plastic red shoes. They were as bright as a firetruck and sized for an elephant. The customs agent regarded Camden with confusion. A question formed on his lips. Camden was suddenly concerned that he might have to explain something in French. He kicked himself for not bothering to learn the word for "clown." But the customs agent's indifference won out before any communication commenced. The question conveniently vanished from his lips.

Camden passed through customs and entered Africa. As his first official act, he decided to have another go at finding a toilet. Sailing through customs without incident had a soothing effect that extended to the bowling ball lodged in his bowels. But as he spotted the bathroom sign, a ruckus erupted behind him. There were shouts. There was shuffling. A group of soldiers nearly knocked him over as they rushed past with machine guns drawn. Camden spun around and saw them converge on the customs desk where Lukas, red-faced and top hat askew, was standing.

His suitcase was open on the customs desk. The customs agent held in one hand a long thin dagger that he had removed from the suitcase. In the other, the agent held a revolver, that pointed between Lukas's eyes.

4

After his goats were barbequed on the Wanda Road, Jammu saw no reason to go back to Unubi. Without his flock, Nana's family would never allow her to marry him. Teacher Mapouro was the richest man in the village and enjoyed all the advantages of land, livestock, and satellite television. Compared to him, Jammu had nothing – not even two good feet. Jammu had been laughed out of Unubi once. He had no intention of experiencing that humiliation again, only to see Nana wed to another. "Why would Nana marry you?" the townspeople would snicker to Jammu, as if the answer was too obvious to be cruel. Unfortunately, he would have no good reply.

Jammu turned away from Unubi and followed the Wanda Road deeper into the savanna. The fertile highlands to the east disappeared behind the horizon. He travelled through an unfamiliar and unforgiving plain. The land became drier, the grass browner, and the trees scrubbier. The land was the color of a corpse. The sun was a rotten orange. Eventually, even the vultures abandoned Jammu. His only companion on his desolate walkabout was his last goat, which followed faithfully on his heels.

Joined by his goat, he drifted down the road like a lost soul, without any destination, food, or water. Jammu didn't mind the hunger so much. He had been hungry many times before. But thirst was something that one can never get used to. Sustenance was not a problem for the little goat though. As they travelled, the goat ate everything: grass, shrubs, small stones. The goat even nibbled on the frames of deserted shacks they passed along the way. For his shaggy companion, the Wanda Road was a veritable buffet, a Sizzler of the savanna.

As they limped along, Jammu's body ached. With every step, his clubfoot felt like it was slowly being squeezed in a vice. To ignore the pain, Jammu let his mind wander. Driven by thirsty thoughts, he recalled an old wives' tale that a man could drink water from any source, no matter how dirty, as long as he did not drink for more than three seconds. Jammu had never been thirsty enough to put the advice into action. But as the afternoon sun beat down, he decided that it was worth a try. Jammu knelt beside his little goat, which was lapping at a filthy puddle in the road. As he brushed aside a blanket of flies, Jammu had a moment's hesitation, but he went for it anyway. He regretted his decision as soon as his lips touched the muck.

He walked through the night. By morning, a town had risen out of darkness to the west. But Jammu was dizzy with thirst and too busy running his sandpaper tongue over his cracked lips to notice. By the afternoon, he was no longer aware of the road, the savanna, or even the loyal goat by his side. His eyesight narrowed and dimmed. With his perspective reduced to a pinhole, memories of Nana danced in his tunnel vision, crowding out everything else. There was playful Nana, laughing and skipping as she dashed between the mango trees. A diligent Nana balancing a bundle of cassava on her head. Chaste and virtuous Nana washed the pale bottoms of her feet in the river. As Jammu stumbled along, these memories became prospective, shifting from things that had been to what might be. Nana became his wife. He imagined a little shack. He imagined harder and saw a big house with his own satellite dish on the roof. He saw a child in that house. Then he saw many children, multiplying in his fertile fantasies. His head swam with hallucinations of Nana, bathing him in grace. Without realizing it, he had stopped walking. Gravity became an irresistible drag as he slumped to the road.

Jammu was set to spend the rest of his short life on the Wanda Road, dreaming of what would never be, until a noise shook him from his sweetly suicidal trance. There was a droning in the distance, a faint buzzing in the sky. The noise grew steadily louder. Its volume built to a roar. Jammu craned his neck back to see what had interrupted his delirium. The sudden movement sent aloft a fly that had been strolling across his eyeball. As he looked up, Jammu felt heat on his face. Exhaust fumes burnt his nose. The slipstream from a landing airplane knocked him over.

Jammu struggled to his unsteady feet. In his stupor he had wandered next to an airport runway. A shabby terminal sat at the far end of the tarmac. Beyond the terminal, Jammu finally noticed the town that had lurked on the horizon all morning. Until that moment, he had no idea that a place called Mbanza existed. He glanced down the Wanda Road, which twisted deeper towards nowhere. He looked back at the town. He left the road and made a beeline for Mbanza.

Although he did not think it possible, Jammu discovered that there were even worse ways to travel than the Wanda Road. Trudging cross-country, he waded through waist-deep elephant grass and wait-a-bits that shredded his pants. He crossed a pumice field formed by ancient volcanoes. The heat blistered stone scraped his feet and sent pain shooting up his bad leg. He navigated through squat bushes that dotted the plain like herds of wild porcupine. Any of them might contain snakes, lions, or some other feral thing that would love to have Jammu for lunch. Passing a particularly ominous-looking acacia, Jammu morbidly considered whether he'd rather die a slow death of snake venom, or a quick and terrible death of being mauled by a lion. He saw little upside to either possibility. Suddenly feeling very exposed, Jammu sought consolation in his only companion. He could not see the little goat, but the tall grass swayed by his side to the sound of ruminate chewing. Jammu reached below the grass and rubbed the goat's bony head like a lucky rabbit's foot.

The town was close now, and Jammu could make out more detail. Objectively, it was not a large town, but to Jammu, who was born in Unubi and spent better the part of his adolescence in a goat pasture, it might as well have been Manhattan. On the top of a hill sat some old colonial buildings. Below it, a slum was scattered across the plain like shards of broken pottery. The spaces between the shacks were less like streets than rivers of red dirt that meandered between the haphazard construction of repurposed wood and used oil drums. In the town, only one building stood out, both in terms of its height and its architectural intentionality. Set apart from the town on a slightly smaller hill sat a tower of concrete and glass with a green neon marquee on top. Standing at six stories, the Hotel Internationale was five stories taller than any building Jammu had seen before. He stumbled towards the tower, drawn like a termite to a street light.

Jammu was a simple boy. He knew goats. He knew he loved Nana. And his understanding of the world basically stopped there. As he gazed onto the hotel terrace, nothing in his humble existence could have prepared him for the resort-like amenities of the Hotel Internationale. He saw men of many races reclining in lounge chairs, eating and drinking and laughing. The pool was bluer than any jewel he could imagine. If he had seen the lazy river or the plinko machines, he probably would have had some sort of religious experience. The Hotel Internationale seemed to him like Xanadu in its pleasure palace proportions and he imagined that among such plenty, there must be room for a boy and his goat.

Delirious with thirst and pumped up by the Senegalese pop blaring over the outdoor sound system, Jammu flailed towards the entrance. His manic approach caught the attention of a middle-aged porter in a starchy wool bellhop uniform that might have made sense in St. Moritz, but not the savanna. The porter leveled his eyes on Jammu and decided at once that neither Jammu nor his goat were Hotel Internationale material. Assuming the full dignity of a man with little authority, the porter marched towards Jammu, flicking his hands as one might shoo a dog. When Jammu had the temerity to ask for water, the porter started to swing a broom, which finally got the point across. Filled with the satisfaction of a job well done, the porter watched the boy and his goat scurry away down the road towards Mbanza.

5

Hours later, Olson still had a bad taste in his mouth. It was like the aftertaste of sour milk. Bad shellfish. Or orange juice and toothpaste. This sensation was Olson's usual reaction to Laurent Congolo. Congolo, along with the rest of Mbanza's government organs, was as corrupted as a diseased colon. But it spoke volumes that one meeting could have such a profound effect on Olson, an experienced professional jaundiced by years of professional deception and native spirits.

After leaving the Hotel Internationale, Olson spent the afternoon helping Kruger load the shipment. Olson kept his weapons cache, the lethal goodies that he parceled out to the Mbanzan government, hidden in a clandestine warehouse outside the city. To avoid unwanted attention, the warehouse had no electricity, which helped keep the location secret but also meant there was no air conditioning. In Olson's opinion, whoever called machine guns "light" arms had obviously never moved crates of them in an airless cinder block bunker with a tin roof.

Before coming to Mbanza, Olson never did his own heavy lifting. In a normal country, the hard work could be sourced to local labor under the cover of a generic import-export business. But Mbanza was not a normal country. Years of war and famine had left their mark. There was nothing that was not worth stealing. If anyone found out about the warehouse, it would be cleared out in a day. If anyone realized that it contained thousands of dollars of not-so-light arms, munitions, medical supplies, and one antiquated, but more or less functional tank, the place would be stripped in minutes.

Trying to ignore the suffocating heat and a cellphone blowing up his pocket, Olson loaded the last crate into the supply truck. Trusting Kruger to handle the delivery, Olson returned to Mbanza. It was dusk when he reached his office. On the edge of the city where the old town on the hill spilled onto the slums below, Olson turned down an anonymous alley and stopped at a non-descript door. A sign hung above the door, barely legible in the darkness. It read: "The Fistula Initiative."

Olson had never gotten used to his cover. There were many unpleasant aspects of his current posting, but the regular reminder of fistulas was a uniquely icky one. Olson had never been one for gore. The mere mention of blood caused every knuckle and joint in his body to throb arthritically. Although his job presented messy moral situations – absolute abortions from an ethical perspective – the tradecraft itself would be a largely bloodless affair. When practiced properly, it was virtually antiseptic. Causes were uncertain. Effects could be rationalized. Responsibility could be shirked. And Olson had always left by the time the shooting started anyway.

But this convenient arrangement did not hold true Mbanza. Nothing was neat or clean. The whole country was a weeping sore. It was fitting that his cover involved something as awful as fistula. It went with the theme. And, at the end of the day, Olson could not deny that it was a good cover. The Fistula Initiative was an elegant solution to avoiding unwanted attention. Whenever he told anyone where he worked and described the condition in even general terms, the subject was promptly changed. No one asked follow-up questions. And no one ever stopped by for a surprise visit.

Olson entered the office and passed through the waiting area, which consisted of a dust-covered reception desk and a coffee table littered with thalidomide-era World Health Organization reports on reproductive health. He walked into the back. Several offices and storage rooms lined a hallway that terminated at a set of stairs. If he had his druthers, Olson would have marched up those stairs, poured a glass of rum, rinsed the taste of Congolo from his mouth, and crawled into bed. But there was more work to do. His life was like a backed-up septic tank. The shit never cleared.

"Is that you, Olson?" Gary called from down the hall.

"Is it ever anyone else?" Olson answered back.

"I had to ask," Gary said. "Security and all that. Can you come here for a minute?"

Olson found Gary in the operations room, seated behind a large computer terminal and monitor. The operations room looked more like the back of a bankrupt Best Buy than a command center. A single row of fluorescent lights on the ceiling lit the space. Cardboard boxes, loose wires, and assorted hardware cluttered the shelving along the walls. Computers and satellite uplinks sat on desks in varying stages of assembly. With the exception of Gary's station, nothing seemed to work.

Gary reclined in an office chair with a controller in his lap. His big cheeks and pale face were fitting for a man who spent most of the day in a dark room behind a computer screen. A bowl of instant ramen sat to his left on the desk. An open jar of peanut butter to his right.

"Why didn't you pick up your phone?" Gary asked. "I was trying to reach you for hours."

"I was getting lunch at the Hotel," Olson said.

"You were eating all afternoon? How many rum and cokes did that involve?"

"It wasn't that kind of lunch. I was busy with something," Olson elaborated unhelpfully, "I had things to do. People to see. Need to know stuff."

"We're a team," Gary said, wincing with concentration at the monitor. "What you know, I need to know."

"We are not on the same team, Gary. We just live in the same building. We share a kitchen. But that's the extent of it. You stick to the drones. And I do, well, whatever it is I do."

"Come off it," Gary said. "We work for the same agency. I have the same clearances that you do."

"I know they give out clearances like candy these days, but I trade in secrets," Olson said. "And the only way to keep a secret between two people is if one of them is dead. Unless you want me to have to kill you, don't ask about my day. Or my lunches."

"Secrets, secrets," Gary groaned. "Okay, keep your precious secrets. But if we're going to be compartmentalized about everything, I guess I can't tell you about the persons of interest that I identified this afternoon."

Olson had started to leave the room, but the mention of "persons of interest" seized his attention.

"Persons of interest?" he muttered reluctantly. "Okay, I'll bite. Let's hear it."

"I don't' know if I should say," Gary said, setting the controller in his lap to eat some ramen. "It's drone stuff."

"Cut out the crap," Olson said. "Tell me about these interesting persons."

Gary proceeded to recount while shoveling ramen into his face. "Hmm, let's see. I got an eye on two trucks. They were traveling up the Wanda Road. The trucks were loaded with men. And the men were carrying a lot of machine guns."

"Maybe it was just some poachers," Olson said. "Or maybe they were going to a wedding. AK-47s always impress father in-laws."

Gary leaned back his head and slurped down a mouthful of noodles, not unlike a fat baby bird swallowing a worm. "They did seem ready to party," he said when his throat was clear of ramen. "They had a .50 caliber gun mounted onto one of the trucks."

"That is a lot of fireworks," Olson agreed.

"And I'm just talking about the equipment," Gary said. "They were also acting in a very anti-social manner. I saw them take out a civilian. They dropped him right in the middle of the road. Then they stole his goats. It was cold."

"Goat thieves with AK-47s? I was wrong to doubt you. These are extremely interesting people," Olson said. "Why didn't you let me know about this earlier?"

"I tried to call," Gary said. "Repeatedly. You didn't pick up."

"Well, I'm here now," Olson said. He started to walk around the terminal to see Gary's screen. "Is the situation live? Do you have eyes on the targets?"

Gary raised his ramen in protest. "Hey, wait a minute. You can't look at this screen!"

"Why" Olson asked with a thin grin. "We have the same clearances. Remember? Now point that ramen somewhere else and let me . . ." Olson trailed off. As he saw the screen, his grin sagged like the wet noodle dangling from Gary's fork.

"Gary, what's on the screen?" Olson asked dryly. "This doesn't look like Africa. This doesn't even look like planet Earth. I might be wrong, but Africans don't usually have laser rifles, right?"

Since arriving in Mbanza six months before, Gary's waking hours had been devoted to one of two things: flying drones and playing Xbox. Currently, Gary was playing Xbox. Halo to be exact.

"Why aren't you monitoring the targets?" Olson asked, his patience thin and weary.

"Because the mission ended an hour ago," Gary said.

"How did it end?"

"With a liquidation."

Olson was visibly annoyed. "You liquidated without me? You know I have to review these things. Procedure, Gary!"

"Answer your phone next time. You choose your own involvement," Gary said. He set aside his ramen and picked up his controller. An alien on the screen promptly drove a glowing purple sword through a metal man's head. "Whenever you're ready to review, the video is uploaded to the server. But I guess I've spoiled the ending."

Olson turned to go. Gary interrupted his exit a second time.

"Hey, if you go out again, can you pick up some milk?"

"And why can't you go out?" Olson asked.

"Because my job is here. With the computers. One of us has to hold down the fort."

"Maybe you should turn off the video games and interact with the world."

"It's too hot to go outside. And I can't understand a word anyone says. Besides, they pay me to drop bombs on people – not talk to them. If I got too friendly with the locals, I might not be able to do my job."

Leaving Gary to the Xbox, Olson retreated to his office and collapsed into his chair. He tossed his cell phone onto his desk and returned his beard to the drawer where he kept a Clouseau-esque collection of disguises, which included sunglasses, hair pieces, fake noses, and the like. As he logged onto his computer, he made a cocktail with his free hand. He pulled a bottle of Tipo Tipico rum from the shelf and mixed it with some warm mango juice.

Olson took a long sip as the computer connected to the secure network. He opened his email and sorted through the administrative fluff that cluttered his inbox. With an index finger parked on the "delete" button, Olson dispatched the hordes of inter-agency spam – notices about blood drives, financial boot camps, diversity training, and "Cookie Thursdays" – that meant little to anyone in headquarters and absolutely nothing to an agent in the field. He was looking for a reply to a report that he had sent last week. The report included gossip about power-jockeying in the middle rungs of the government and some unsubstantiated intelligence about rebel troop movements. While not part of his official duties, the report was an element of his multi-prong campaign to: first, get back in the agency's good graces; second, get the hell out of Africa; and, third, not go insane with boredom.

The scope of Olson's African assignment was as restrictive as a straight-jacket. He arranged weapons shipments to the Mbanzan government and made sure that those weapons were used on the right people. While gun running might sound exciting to the uninitiated, the reality was not nearly as sexy as advertised. When he wasn't loading crates in stuffy warehouses, Olson was sitting on the savanna with binoculars, sweating bullets and counting explosions. It was dull, hot, soul crushing work. It didn't do his mental health any favors either. If there was a more tedious way of developing PTSD than watching explosions all day, he did not want to know about it.

But back to the inbox.

Olson did not find a reply to his report. He checked the spam folder just to be safe. Unfortunately, he was not surprised. HQ never contacted him about anything substantive anymore. He was obviously being ignored. The silence was too complete to not be intentional. Statistically-speaking, he should have been included on an email chain from time to time, if only by accident.

At least a blind cc.

After all, Olson had been assigned to Mbanza – a dusty little nowhere that not even Bono could give two shits about – for a reason. He still cringed when he thought about Benghazi, the botched operation that resulted in his professional exile. Olson never denied that Benghazi had not gone as planned. If a few stiff drinks and some stiffer arm twisting were applied, he'd admit that it had been a total disaster. But there was not enough rum in Mbanza to make Olson believe that Benghazi had actually been his fault. He hadn't done anything wrong. Maybe he had not done exactly what HQ asked him to do, but he had done everything right. If they wanted blind obedience, they could replace him with a robot. No mission ever went according to plan perfectly: there was always an element of improvisation. The countless times his missions had been successful, HQ never complained about the creative impulses he exhibited in completing the mission. But after one little international incident, HQ wanted to crucify him. And, at the end of the day, who in his line of work hadn't stumbled into a crisis? If there was an agent out there who hadn't had their own Benghazi, let them cast the first stone.

Some days – every day, actually – Olson wished they'd just fired him. He constantly fantasized about leaving Africa for good. But Olson stuck good and proper. HQ would never fire him. He was too valuable as a linguist. Half his so-called colleagues could hardly speak English, let alone another foreign language.

47

No, they'd hang him out to dry, but they wouldn't cut the string. And Olson would never quit either. He was good at his job, and, frankly, he didn't know what else he would do. There was no way to win. The was no off ramp. Mbanza was a hell of a place to be left out in the cold.

As Olson neared the miserable end of his cocktail, a new message flashed into the empty inbox. He blinked for a moment, unable to believe his eyes. From the subject line, he could see that it was HQ's reply to his report. He threw back his drink with a fortifying swig, grimacing at the taste. He opened the email. The message burned worse than the cheap rum.

There was a one sentence reply: "Shouldn't you be counting explosions?

Olson closed his email and suppressed the desire to throw his computer across his office. After mixing another rum cocktail, he picked up a week-old newspaper from the capital. He immediately regretted his decision. In between puff pieces about government victories and rebel setbacks were unsettling tales of true crime, Mbanza-style. Below the fold was a story about some villagers who had burned alive twin sisters accused of witchcraft. Elsewhere, a decapitated head was found next to a gas station. Coincidently, but unrelated, a headless body was discovered outside a government office. Page two was dominated by news of yet another albino murder. Mbanza, like other countries in the region, had an unhealthy trade in albino parts, driven by the insane belief that its pale-skinned countrymen had medicinal hearts, magical livers, and bones made of gold. Olson knew people could be superstitious, but the albino business boggled the mind. He had no idea how that degree of ignorance persisted. The first time anyone actually murdered an albino, the myth of the gold bones should have been definitively busted. He could only imagine the disappointment of anyone who ever cut into one of those poor bastards, only to discover that they were filled with the same blood and guts as everyone else. But, despite this inevitable moment of reckoning, the myth persisted. And a grainy photograph in newsprint testified to that fact. Disgusted, he threw the newspaper into the trash.

Looking for a less gruesome distraction, Olson emptied the rest of the Tipo Tipico into his glass and turned on Gary's drone footage from that afternoon. His job was to know things, so he had to watch it sooner or later. And while the video was essentially a military-grade snuff film, it bothered him less than the newspaper. The video was taken at altitude, which tamped down the gore and created an acceptable psychic distance. Olson settled back in his chair and observed a drone's-eye view of two trucks bounding down a long dirt road. The perspective reminded him OJ Simpson's white Ford Bronco. Between the fuzzy feeling of the rum, and his exhaustion from the afternoon, he was asleep in minutes.

The cell phone's buzzing woke Olson. Groggily, he lifted his head off his desk. His cheek was wet. He first thought he spilled his drink. But his glass of rum was still upright. Olson fingered the moisture on his cheek and was relieved that it was just drool.

The phone continued to vibrate. Olson had no idea what time it was. He could have been asleep for a minute or a day. He answered without bothering to look at the caller ID. He listened and said very little. It was a short call.

When the call was over, Olson glanced at the computer. The video was still going. The two trucks were still bumping down a road to nowhere. He let the video run.

Olson tiptoed down the hall past the operations room. He wanted to avoid another conversation with Gary. The sound of gunfire and explosions spilled out of the room. He assumed that Gary was still playing Xbox, but honestly, who the hell knew.

6

Electricity was as scarce a resource as any other in Mbanza. The nightly blackouts did not so much roll as smother the town like a thick, wet blanket. When the sun went down, the people of Mbanza went home, shuttered their windows, and bolted their doors. The streets became a lawless place where no law-abiding person with a drop of sanity chose to be. That is unless such a person had a bulletproof SUV.

As it turned out, Olson was just such a person. While "love" or "like" would have been too strong, he could almost "tolerate" Mbanza at night. Without the people or the oppressive heat, the town was almost inoffensive. And thanks to an eight-cylinder engine and the miracles of armor plating, Olson had free run of it. The roads were clear. There was no creeping behind mango carts or weaving between shit-caked cattle. Olson could open the throttle and approach speeds of 30 – even 35 – miles per hour, a land speed record on Mbanza's main road, which was more or less one long pothole.

The SUV roared through Mbanza like a wheeled demon. Its headlights sliced through the darkness, reflecting off the glinting eyes of dogs, rats, cats, and criminally-inclined that braved the night. But those eyes only flickered for a moment before their owners jumped for safety, narrowly avoiding the SUV's merciless bumper. Because the SUV did not slow down. Olson never slowed down. He cracked the window and felt the wind in his hair. He gripped the steering wheel tightly. A herd of horsepower galloped within his grasp.

The SUV followed the road as it twisted through the slum and climbed the hill to the antebellum old town. The dirt road narrowed and became flecked with cobble stones. As the SUV gained elevation, the shanties in the slum below were replaced by slightly-less decrepit colonial architecture. The SUV creeped among the sagging facades – all faded stucco, dandruffed plaster, and frowning verandas. The old town had certainly seen better times. But even in its heyday, it had only passed for civilization if one squinted hard enough. Mbanza had always been less destination than termination, the last stop on the colonial road before one reached the tattered edge of the map. It was the coda of progress. The cul-de-sac of empires.

Once it reached the top of the hill, the SUV rumbled onto a broad plaza. The headlights illuminated a statue in the center of the square – a monument to Mbanza's independence. Immortalized in bronze, the country's founder and own resident Robert Mugabe wore a benevolent smile and extended his arm in an apparent attempt to give the world a high-five. At his feet knelt two Africans swaddled in loin cloths, brandishing spears and leather shields, struggling to free their legs from blocks of concrete. Taken out of its specific historical context, the monument might have represented two Zulus that ran afoul of a mob run by Morgan Freeman.

Olson drove around the statue and continued across the plaza. The police station was located in an old palazzo, crowned with floodlights and ringed with sand bags and chicken wire. The hum and whiff of diesel generators wafted through the SUV's open windows. Olson approached the perimeter checkpoint where two gaunt soldiers slouched against a machine gun nest. He slowed down and flashed the high beams. An older and appreciably fatter man in an officer's uniform staggered out of a guardhouse, wiping sleep from his eyes. He took one look at Olson's white face and waved him forward. Whatever the police were guarding against, it was not Olson.

He parked the SUV and entered the police station. The lobby was deserted. A row of plastic seats stood along one where a couple of stray dogs had bedded down for the night. They made noises in their throats and kicked from time to time as if chasing dream rabbits. Across the lobby, a duty officer slept at the front desk, snoring softly behind a sneeze guard of bullet proof glass. Olson let the sleeping guard lie and slipped into the back of the station.

Vacant desks were cluttered with paper files, manila folders, and official forms in triplicate. Cycles of disaster, both natural and man-made, had indefinitely

51

delayed the computer revolution in Mbanza, which was still in a pristine, pre-Netscapian state. Somewhere in the station, beyond a phalanx of metal filing cabinets, a voice crackling with static announced a soccer game on a radio. Olson didn't see anyone until he reached the steel door leading to the holding cells. He unbarred the door, which groaned as it swung open. Olson entered the detention area and nearly stepped on a guard. The guard was asleep across the floor with a cigarette burning between his lips. Olson nudged him with his foot. The guard jerked awake, scattering cigarette ash across his shirt as he lunged for his rifle. After a few tense moments and a lot of explanation in French, the guard composed himself and led Olson down the corridor.

On the way to the interrogation room, Olson passed a row of cells. The jail was cramped and crowded, as usual. If a police state was good for nothing else, it was increasing the prison population. A few fortunate prisoners had secured spots on butcherblock bunks. The unlucky majority lined the floor, crammed together like cigars at the bottom of a box. As Olson followed the guard, he glanced absentmindedly at the faces behind the bars. But if he had looked more closely, he might have recognized a familiar face.

Unrice had had an up and down day. On the negative side of the ledger, he was in jail. On the plus side, he was lucky enough to have a bunk. As a result, he had the luxury of considering his predicament from the relative comfort of a moldy mattress. Just that morning, Unrice was on the verge of convincing a rich foreigner to give him thousands of dollars – a sum that would have been enough to start a life somewhere far from Mbanza. But by nightfall, his dream had gone up in smoke. He was in a cell with common criminals, petty thieves, and even murders. He could hardly process the sinister turn. It seemed so unfair. Fortune's corkscrews left him dizzy.

Making matters worse, Unrice had to face these cruel twists alone. Although Elba was lying beside him on the mattress, he had not spoken since their arrest. Granted, the plan to cheat the foreigner had been Unrice's idea and Elba had been a reluctant participant, but Unrice thought his friend was overdoing the silent treatment. Unrice told him the blame game would get them nowhere. But Elba refused to listen to good sense. Consequently, Unrice was left to his own devices. He stared into the hall beyond the cell bars, casting about for a way out of the situation, when the rich foreigner from that afternoon strolled by. Unrice couldn't believe his eyes. Ibrahim wasn't wearing his sunglasses and his beard was gone, but Unrice recognized him immediately. After all, he had never met a foreigner before that afternoon.

Unrice shook Elba by the shoulder. "Wake up. It's the rich foreigner from this morning. It's Ibrahim!"

Elba did not respond. He muttered to himself and curled into a disgruntled ball as he feigned sleep. Unrice saw that Elba would be no help. As usual, he would need to do everything for both of them.

Unrice slipped off the bunk and tiptoed over the men snoring on the floor. "Hey, over here! Ibrahim, it is me Unrice!" he hissed in French through the iron bars.

After an afternoon of gunrunning and an evening of Tipo Tipico, Olson had forgotten about the operation that day. He stopped and stared at the African in the cell, who addressed him in French and called him Ibrahim. He did not recognize Unrice at first. But the filthy farm fingers grasping the cell bars jogged his memory.

"Ibrahim, I don't know what you're doing here," Unrice said, "But you have to help me. The police think that I'm some kind of criminal. You must tell that I am innocent!"

Now that Olson recognized the man behind the bars, he wished he hadn't made eye contact. In a small city like Mbanza, these encounters sometimes occurred. The conversations were always exhausting.

"You're not a criminal?" Olson asked half-heartedly. He barely had the energy that night for the kabuki. "What were you talking about today then? Didn't you say you had connections? That you knew bandits and terrorists?"

"Yes, I said those things. But what was I supposed to do?" Unrice said. "There was so much money on the table. I would have sworn I knew the devil if you'd asked me. You must believe me though, I'm no terrorist! I'm just a farmer, a simple man with wives and children. You have to help me, brother!"

It was late. Olson had work to do. The guard was getting impatient too. He lifted his rifle butt in a bludgeonsome manner. Olson decided to do a good deed by cutting the conversation short and saving Unrice some pain. There would be time enough for that later.

Olson switched from French to Unrice's language – a language he had feigned ignorance of during their first meeting. Olson preferred that the guard not understand their conversation and hoped that Unrice would listen to advice if it was delivered in his own tongue.

"Okay, brother, I do believe you," Olson said, his syllables interspersed with clicks and pops as though he had a mouthful of bubble wrap. "I know you're not a criminal. And the police? They know you're not a criminal too. Everyone knows this. But guess what? No one cares. Take my advice. Just confess."

Unrice was shocked. Both by the blunt advice and the fact that Olson spoke his language. No one outside his tribe – must less a foreigner– spoke his language. Never in a million years would he have imagined that someone would have bothered to learn it.

"But confess to what?" Unrice replied, recovering from his surprise.

"It doesn't matter," Olson said. "Admit to anything they tell you to. They can make you talk. If they have to, they'll hang you upside-down from your toes until the words come out of your mouth. Save yourself the pain. Confess it all. You'll do it sooner or later anyway."

54

On that note, Olson continued down the hall. Unrice was left speechless, clinging to the cell bars by his dirty farm fingers.

The interrogation room was at the end of the cell block. Olson entered. A single lightbulb hung from the ceiling. The darkness and the dank plaster walls gave the impression of a cave. Guards with wooden billy clubs loitered around the room. Olson approached an officer standing in a shadowy corner. It was Lieutenant "So-and-So." They'd met before, but Olson didn't remember his name. This was only fair because the lieutenant didn't know Olson's real name either. The two shook hands.

This was all normal. Olson had been to the police station many times, standing in the shadows, exchanging a few pleasantries before the unpleasant business of interrogation commenced. But things were different this time. The suspects at the table presented a novel twist. Typically, the poor bastards in the hot seat were African. More often than not, by the time Olson arrived, they were well worked-over with a pen in one hand and a confession in the other.

But the three at the table were not the usual suspects. Judging by their white and distinctly non-African faces, they were not local. Moreover, given their lack of superficial bruising and unbroken spirits, no one had evidently laid a finger on them. They weren't beaten, burned, bruised, or electrocuted at all. All the police had done was take away their shoes, which was the gentlest hobbling imaginable.

Olson considered the suspects from the shadows. He pegged them for hippie backpackers. From their cargo shorts to their unwashed hair and the not-so-subtle stink of patchouli, the signs were all there. These were the kind of people that hacky-sacked through Prague, squatted on the beaches in Barcelona, and bought sticky black balls of incense in Istanbul, mistaking it for hash. Had there been any lingering doubt, one suspect even had a man bun and a pukka shell necklace. Yes, Olson recognized the type. But he didn't understand how they had wound up in Mbanza. Even setting aside the civil war, Mbanza didn't have beaches, safaris, or clubs. The countryside was as dry and as flat as a communion wafer. The only

55

place that anyone might call scenic were the highlands and those were overrun with guerillas. The kinds with guns, not bananas.

Mbanza would not have been Olson's first choice for a spring break. But to each their own.

Lieutenant So-and-So addressed him in French.

"This is only half of them," the lieutenant said. "There are three more in the other room. They arrived at the airport this afternoon. We stopped them at customs. Their bags were searched and we found suspicious items. Wigs. Disguises. Unidentified powders. Bags of balloons. We think this may be a very big deal."

"A big deal? How so?" Olson asked.

"For one thing, drug smuggling," the lieutenant said. "We think they may have used the balloons to swallow drugs. We gave them a bucket." He gestured to a yellow plastic bucket in the corner. There was a cartoon deer printed on the side. The deer was Bambi. "They haven't used the bucket yet," he continued. "But they will. Sooner or later, everyone uses the bucket. And when they do, we will be watching."

"Well, that's one possibility. But what did they have to say for themselves?" Olson asked, skeptical of the lieutenant's theory. If a couple of hippies wanted to sell drugs, traveling to a humanitarian disaster zone to set up shop seemed like a backwards way of going about it.

"I have no idea," the lieutenant said with a shrug. "I don't speak English. And they don't speak French."

"I hope you didn't drag me out here because you found some balloons in someone's suitcase," Olson said. "I'm a busy man."

"The balloons are only the start of it. There is much more," the lieutenant said proudly. "They had weapons too. They obviously intended some sort of violence. We found knives. Of many shapes and sizes. And we found this sword. Henri, bring over the sword!"

On his command, one of the guards who had been polishing a billy club brought over the so-called sword. Olson was no expert, but he saw at once that it was some sort of toy or prop. It had the shape and size of a sword, but its blade was dull and it had a cheap plastic handle. Olson doubted that it could cut through butter, much less a throat. Given a decade of civil war, the Mbanza police were justifiably sensitive to security threats. But the only violence this weapon might ever see would be a community theater production of *The Taming of the Shrew*.

The lieutenant elaborated on his theory. "We think they might be a revolutionary cell. We have been in contact with Mr. Laurent Congolo in the Department of Justice. He said that you would be very interested in an operation of this importance. He also asked me to tell you something."

"And what is that?" Olson asked.

"He asked me to tell you that these criminals are surely worth a tank."

"I'm sure he did," Olson said. "Have these criminals talked to anyone else? Does anyone know they're here?"

"Of course not," the lieutenant laughed. "I know the protocol. They are completely off the books. We could make them disappear in a second. God would not know where to find them.

With the briefing completed, the interrogation began. Olson, still holding the prop sword, and Lieutenant So-and-So emerged from the shadows and joined the suspects at the table. Olson took the opportunity to examine the suspects more closely.

The punk with the pukka shells and the manbun was leaning back in his chair with his arms crossed. He wore a smug confidence like a knight wore armor. Olson disliked him immediately.

A skinny girl in the middle balanced on the edge of her seat like a ginger-headed gargoyle. Between her leopard print yoga pants, red hair, and the suggestive way she sucked her lower lip between her teeth, she reminded Olson of an over-sexualized Raggedy Ann doll.

The last suspect had mouse-brown hair and a weak chin. Of the three, he was the only one who seemed to understand the situation and was appropriately scared shitless.

Jody, Piper, and Camden regarded Olson with a mixture of defiance, fear, and, to some degree, hope. Olson was the first non-African they'd seen since their arrest.

The interrogation room was silent. Each side of the table sized up the other.

"Do you speak English?" Piper asked, dipping her toe into the waters of conversation.

"Yes, I speak English," Olson replied with professional coolness.

Despite his dispassionate tone, the group was encouraged by a response in a language they understood. The conversational floodgates opened. Words spilled forth.

"Thank god!" Piper exclaimed. "You've got to help us. We've been in here for hours!"

"They won't even take us to the bathroom. They expect us to use a bucket!" Camden said with personal grievance.

"We demand to speak to the embassy. You can't treat us like this!" Jody declared. He stood up as though the indignity of detention was not something he could take sitting down.

"It would be a good idea if you got back in that seat," Olson said, stifling a yawn. The protest did not impress him.

"And what if I don't?" Jody said. "What are you going to do? Arrest me?"

"I'm not going to do anything," Olson said. He gestured towards the guards with the billy clubs. "But they will. The police have a way of making you sit. They break your toes. They're good at it. I've seen them do it before. You already have your shoes off. You're halfway there."

"Are you trying to intimidate me?" Jody replied. The question was meant to sound defiant, but there was uncertainty in his voice. "We have rights."

"In this country?" Olson asked. "Who put that silly idea in your head?"

A staring competition followed. Jody glared down at Olson. Olson looked back at Jody with tired eyes. In the force of wills, Jody was the first to blink. He took his seat – albeit with a humph.

"That's better," Olson said. "Now let's have a chat." Olson considered the suspects. He didn't like any of them. But if he wanted answers, he had to talk to someone. For a lack of better options, Olson pointed to the one who annoyed him the least.

"You, what's your name?" Olson asked.

"Me? My name is Camden," he answered, startled by the finger aimed at him.

"Okay, Camden. You talk. Everyone else listen. If you all talk at once, I won't understand a damn thing. And that will be bad for you. Got it?"

The suspects understood, although Jody was clearly annoyed that he had not been elected to speak for the group. He did not give up the cloak of leadership lightly.

"Let's take this one step at a time," Olson said. "Tell me what you did to end up in the back of a police station?"

"We didn't do anything. I swear," Camden said.

"Really? The police here don't arrest people for no reason," Olson said, knowing from personal experience this was a big fat lie.

"But Cammy's telling the truth," Piper interrupted. "We just arrived today. We didn't have time to do anything!"

"What's your name?" Olson asked.

"Piper."

"Be quiet, Piper," Olson said. "This isn't your turn to talk. Did you ever go to summer camp? You look like the type of person who went to summer camp. Let's pretend that Camden has the talking stick. It's his turn to talk – not yours. Now, Camden, you just got to the airport today? Let me be the first to welcome you to Africa. You and your friends wasted no time getting into trouble."

"This is all a really big misunderstanding," Camden said.

"That's certainly possible," Olson agreed. "There is a language barrier. If you don't speak French, it is hard to explain why you're carrying a suitcase filled with knives through the airport." To focus the conversation, Olson set the sword on the table. "I hope you can understand why lethal weapons like these might make the police curious."

"Lethal weapons?" Jody scoffed. "They're just props, bro. They're toys!"

Olson took a deep breath. His patience was wearing thin. And so was Lieutenant So-and-So, who was not accustomed to being interrupted during his own interrogations. The officer's face flushed the color of red velvet cake as he reached for the pistol on his belt. Olson tapped his arm and shook his head.

Ignoring Jody, Olson returned to questioning Camden.

"Is that true? Is this just a toy? Why was it in your bag?"

"It wasn't in *my* bag," Camden said. "It was in Lukas's bag. He's the tall Dutch guy they have in the other room."

"His bag. Your bag. Now is not the time for semantics. You're all in this together," Olson said.

"But Lukas is basically a stranger. I only met him yesterday. Same with the two Bulgarian girls. They're Jody's friends," Camden said, eager to shift whatever blame could. "Not mine."

"But you came here as a group," Olson said. "They arrested you all at the airport together."

"But we're not together. Not really," Camden insisted. Nervous sweat beaded on his forehead. "They're just here for the festival too."

Olson opened his lips to ask about this "festival," but Jody, eager to wrest back the cloak of leadership from Camden, asserted himself.

"If we're being questioned, shouldn't we have a lawyer?" he asked.

"Do I look like a lawyer referral service?" Olson asked.

"What are you doing here then? You're from the embassy, right?"

60

"No, I'm not from the embassy," Olson said.

"If you're not from the embassy, who are you?" Jody asked.

"I'm the man who askes the questions," Olson said.

"Listen man, I'm not going to play your games," Jody said. "I don't respond to jackboot tactics. Don't I get a phone call?"

"You aren't getting a phone call," Olson said.

"I want a phone call!" Jody insisted.

Olson took a deep breath and massaged the bridge of his nose. He spoke deliberately, trying to suppress the desire to choke Jody with his own pukka shell necklace.

"You are not getting a phone call," Olson said. "First, there aren't any working telephones in the station. And I'm not going to let you breathe all over my cell phone. Second, even if there was a phone, the police aren't going to let you use it. Let me explain things because you obviously don't understand your situation. You have no rights here. No one knows where you are. Not your parents. Not the embassy. You are standing on the edge of a world of hurt. I am your lifeline here. I am your port in the storm. I am the only thing keeping those guards from popping you like a pimple. And if you think the popping is the bad part, you have clearly never experienced the pleasures of spending the night in a general population cell in a least developed country. You three will be the prettiest things that these hardened criminals have ever seen."

Olson's speech had its intended effect. Jody's lips, and rectum, pursed shut.

With Jody silenced, at least momentarily, Camden continued. "This is all a huge misunderstanding," he said, grimacing with a mixture of desperation and constipation. "We're a bunch of clowns."

"Oh, I can see that," Olson said.

"No, really," Camden said. "We're actually clowns. Like in the circus."

"Speak for yourself," Jody said, recovering his powers of speech. "I've never clowned in my life. I'm an acro-yoga artist."

61

"Jesus, Jody. Give it a rest," Camden said. He turned back to Olson. "Seriously, mister, you have to believe us. If you just let me have my bag, I'll show you."

There was some luggage sitting in the corner of the interrogation room. Olson motioned for Camden's suitcase. A guard brought it over and set it on the table. Before Camden opened it, Olson offered some advice. "Just take it nice and slow. These guards are jittery and very poorly trained. Don't make any fast movements."

Camden nodded. He opened the suitcase like a sloth unpacking from vacation. Delicately, as if defusing a bomb, he removed a rainbow wig and a pair of oversized red plastic shoes. He placed the wig and the shoes on the table.

Olson considered these items. After a career in intelligence, Olson had thought he knew everything about stupidity. Evidently, he still had some things to learn.

"Okay, let's say I believe you," Olson said. "You're a bunch of clowns. What are you doing in Africa?"

"We've come for the festival," Camden said. "*Cirque du Poverte.*"

"*Cirque du Poverte*? I've never heard of it," Olson said.

"It's a charity thing," Camden added with a shrug.

"A charity thing," Olson repeated with a heavy dose of skepticism.

"It's not *just* a 'charity' thing," Jody said, butting back into the conversation. "It's a major international event. It's supported by the United Nations or something. It's totally a big deal."

"It can't be that big of a deal. I don't know anything about any festival," Olson said. "And it's my job to know things."

"But it is a big deal!" Piper said, adding her voice to the chorus. "Performers are flying in from all around the world. We raised the donations to come here and everything. We raised over $10,000!"

"You raised $10,000 to come here?" Olson asked.

Piper nodded. "We needed it for the flight, our hotel, our registration at the university."

Olson stopped her. "The university? What university are you talking about? There is no university here."

"Sure there is. The Technical University of Mombasa," Camden said. "They're hosting the event."

Olson lifted his hand up. "Wait a second. Did you just say *Mombasa*?"

"Yeah, what about it?" Camden asked.

"You know that you're in *Mbanza*, right?"

"Sheesh, sorry the University of *Mbanza*," Camden corrected himself. "Sorry about my pronunciation."

"No, listen to me closely," Olson said. "You're not following. *Mbanza* and *Mombasa* are two different places. They're in completely different countries. Mombasa is in Kenya. Mbanza is, well, you're in Mbanza. You know that, right?" Olson broke his cool demeanor for the first time during the interrogation. He laughed bitterly and shook his head. "Did you even look at a map? They're not even spelled the same. Didn't you notice that when you bought the tickets?"

Camden looked down at the table. All eyes turned on him. He was the money man. He had planned everything. He had purchased the plane tickets for the group.

"I didn't notice," Camden confessed to the table. "I thought that, well. . . you know, that Mbanza was just the local spelling. And Mombasa was how they spelled it in English."

The room was like a tomb. Camden wilted in his seat. His intestines twisted. His stomach gurgled with shame.

"I guess you really are a clown," Olson said, breaking the silence.

"I juggle too," Camden said feebly.

"And those three in the other room?" Olson asked. "Are they also clowns?"

"Lukas is a sword swallower," Camden said. "The girls are a pair of mimes."

"And your two friends here?"

"They do acro-yoga."

"Acro what?"

"It's acrobatic-yoga," Jody started to explain. "It's the art of . . ."

"I really don't care," Olson said, cutting him off. He took a long sour look at the suspects. The only noise in the room was his fingers impatiently drumming the table.

"I think I've heard enough," Olson said. "I'm pretty sure that you three aren't going to start any trouble here. You're only a danger to yourselves. And that's all I need to know. With any luck, I'll never see any of you again. Let me offer you a piece of advice. Go back to the airport and get the first flight home. Mbanza is not the place for you."

Olson signaled to Lieutenant So-and-So. They both got up to leave the interrogation room. As Olson reached the door, he turned back to Camden.

"Someone really gave you jokers $10,000 to come here?" Olson asked. "For charity?"

"Yes, someone did," Camden said vaguely.

"If you wanted to help someone, you could have just sent the $10,000 to the Red Cross and called it a day."

Camden didn't reply. Coming to Africa had never been his idea anyway. But Jody felt obliged to defend the trip.

"Anyone can send money," he muttered. "We wanted to give people something more important than money. We wanted to share ourselves. We wanted to give our art."

"We wanted to bring joy," Piper added. "And happiness. And hope!"

Olson considered this. "I think people would have rather had the money," he said.

7

It was morning. Jammu slipped off the discarded grass mat that he had repurposed as a blanket. As he rubbed the sleep from his eyes, a half-nude rooster, its midriff revealed by mange, stood atop a neighboring trash heap like the last survivor of some avian apocalypse. Flockless but resolved, it proceeded to crow, announcing the new day.

The rest of Mbanza was waking up along with Jammu. The residents unbarred their windows, threw open their doors, and emptied their bed pans into the sewage canal that wormed through the town like the proverbial shit creek. The red dirt road filled with men pushing carts and wheelbarrows. A corroded pickup truck, painted rust orange and filled with junk, honked its horn as it cut off a man driving a skeletal cow with a car antenna. The rooster on the trash pile, not to be outdone by the truck, crowed louder.

Jammu pulled himself to his feet. A street seller was setting up a stall nearby. The proximity of young goatherds crawling out of trash piles was apparently not considered a damper on business. The stall was hung with knock-off Premier League jerseys, third-hand books, and bootleg DVDs. Jammu approached the stall, drawn by a selection of action movies. He gawked at the plastic cases featuring kung fu masters, comic book supermen, and vintage Jean Claude Van Dammes. The cover of *Delta Force 2: The Colombian Connection* mesmerized him. Chuck Norris's icy gaze. The uzi cradled in the well-oiled bicep. All tastefully framed by a blazing American flag.

The goat interrupted Jammu's groggy fixation on the bad-assery of Chuck Norris. Standing knee deep in the trash, downhill from the rooster crowing its beak off, it bleated happily as it happened upon a rich vein of plantain leaves. Jammu's stomach rumbled as he watched the goat inhale the greasy peels. Having eaten nothing but the Wanda Road's dust for the last two days, he envied the goat's lead belly and uncomplicated tastes. While the goat gorged itself, Jammu scavenged some rope, which he tied around its neck. He felt guilty about depriving the goat of its breakfast, but he needed to eat too, and plantain leaves would not cut it. The little goat put up an outsized resistance as Jammu dragged it from the pile.

Jammu wandered Mbanza in search of food. With the goat pulling at its leash and hunger making his head spin, every step was a struggle. Unfortunately, the effort was hardly worth the trouble. As Jammu walked through the slum, he found no food – only other famished people. Tired men glared at him from open doors. Women supervised empty pots and unlit fires. Children sat in the shade, too weak to play. The whole town waited for the next shipment of rice, which the government delivered with calculated irregularity. The government maintained a delicate nutritional balance in Mbanza by providing just enough food to prevent starvation, but not so much that people would have the surplus calories to cause any trouble.

Occasionally, Jammu passed men hacking half-rotten mangos into slices for sale. But he had no money to pay for the fruit and was afraid to beg. Considering the anger with which these men whacked the fruit, Jammu sensed, quite rightly, that they'd sooner cut off his hand than give him a hand-out. Despite the gnawing emptiness in his belly, he decided not to risk it. Jammu only had three good limbs: he couldn't chance losing another.

The day progressed. The sun climbed higher, along with the temperature. In the morning heat, the sewage canals running through the slum reeked like spoiled mayonnaise. With his bad leg throbbing and the smell of shit tickling his nose, Jammu began to second-guess his decision to come to Mbanza. But just as his spirits began to plumb their lower depths, he discerned a smell other than human waste. A delicious scent wafted from across street. A proper brick building stood there among the shacks. Painted in bright blue letters on white plywood, a sign over the door announced in French: "Praise to the Profit Bakery." Jammu could not read French, but he knew what bread smelled like. He had unwittingly stumbled across the finest – and only remaining – purveyor of savory pies in Mbanza.

Miss Patrice, the proud proprietress, was taking a break outside her bakery. Her dress was covered in a yellow film of unbleached flour. She was a large woman in a lean country, a fact attributable to her keen business sense and rigorous quality control of pies. She breathed deeply and slowly, trying to move as little as possible in the heat as any large mammal on the savanna would do. To pass the time and preserve her dental health, she polished her teeth with a pliable green twig.

Miss Patrice had watched Jammu for some time as he dragged the goat up the street. After living through years of civil war and famine, she had become hardened to suffering. She wasn't selfish exactly, but charity was a luxury she could not afford. That said, Jammu was the most pitiful thing she had seen in some time. He limped unevenly on his club foot. His face was caked with dust and grime. His clothes hung in tatters like filthy garlands on a withered Christmas tree. It was no small feat to make one's suffering stand out in Mbanza, but Jammu nailed it. Still, Miss Patrice's interest in Jammu was not purely humanitarian. He had something that most starving orphans did not have. Namely, a goat.

Jammu followed his nose to where Miss Patrice sat on a stool by the bakery door. He looked her in the eye, too desperate to be anything but direct. "Please give me something to eat," he said. "I'm very hungry."

Miss Patrice stopped polishing her teeth and spat.

"I don't have money. I can work though," Jammu continued. "I can sweep for you. I can carry water. I can do whatever you need. Please just give me whatever you are making. It smells delicious. What is it?" He craned his neck towards the open door. His nostrils flared ravenously. The goat was also enchanted by the aroma of fresh-baked goods and pulled at the rope in Jammu's hand.

"It's pie," Miss Patrice said, shifting on her stool to block the door. "The best meat pie in Mbanza."

"If you give me a piece, I'll do anything you ask," Jammu said. "I haven't eaten in days."

"I have no work for you, boy. I sweep my own floors. I bake my own pies. And I don't need someone to fetch me water. Do I look like I live in the bush? See that spigot?" she said, pointing a thick finger at one of the few working water pumps in town. "The water comes to Miss Patrice. Miss Patrice does not go to the water."

"There must be something you need," he said.

"The only thing I want is money. If I don't get money, you don't get pie."

"But I have just walked all the way across the savanna!"

"Walk across the savanna?" Miss Patrice scoffed. "Why would you do a stupid thing like that?"

"Oh, please. I haven't eaten in three days," Jammu persisted. "Maybe I could sell pies for you? I could deliver them in a cart."

The suggestion made Miss Patrice laugh.

"Oh, I'm sure that you'd like a cart of pies. That would be good for you. But it would be bad for my business. Giving a hungry boy pies would be like letting a fox into a henhouse. Besides, if I wanted someone to deliver my pies, I'd hire someone with two good feet." She shook her twig at his deformed foot. "Sorry, child. If you want one of Miss Patrice's pies, you'll have to pay for it like everyone else."

"But I have nothing to pay with," Jammu said desperately.

Miss Patrice deposited the twig in her mouth and resumed chewing. "Well, I wouldn't say you have nothing," she said, grinding the stick with her molars.

"What do you mean?" Jammu asked. "Look at me. I have no money. My clothes are shredded. I have nothing hidden in my pockets. I don't even have pockets."

Miss Patrice spat and flashed a sly smile.

"You may not have pockets, but you have that animal," she said, gesturing towards the goat, which had never stopped straining at its leash. "My pies are delicious. But it gets harder every day to find good ingredients. I used to make pies

68

of chicken, beef, and lamb. Now I'm lucky to have bushmeat. But that goat would be a delicious filling. He is a little small, but we can fatten him up. I bet we could make, hmm, a dozen pies out of him," Miss Patrice lied, certain the actual number was twice that.

"If that little goat is worth a dozen pies," she continued. "I'll give you one pie now as a finder's fee. Maybe even two. What do you say? Do we have a deal?"

Jammu looked down at the goat pulling at the rope. "But he is all I have in the world," he said. "He is not for pies. He is for Nana."

Miss Patrice shrugged. "The choice is yours, child. You can keep that goat. Or you can eat. But you can't have both." She chomped on her twig, smirking like a bad poker player with a royal flush.

Jammu agonized at the dilemma he faced. His eyes flicked between the goat and the pies visible through the bakery door. His empty stomach gurgled persuasively in favor of the pies. But as Jammu considered the goat, Jammu saw more than an animal. He saw the hope, however faint, of a future with Nana. To give up the goat would be to abandon his true love. The goat was destined for greater things than filling for a pie, no matter how tender and flaky the crust.

To Miss Patrice's disbelief, Jammu dragged his goat away from the bakery without another word. Her jaw went slack and the green twig fell from her lips. She had never seen such resolve in someone so young and so hungry. The example impressed her so much that she almost called Jammu back to reward his conviction with pie. But this charitable urge quickly passed. Miss Patrice was a sensible business woman. The last thing she needed was a reputation as a pushover.

The little goat trotted alongside Jammu, chewing on a tin can and blissfully ignorant that it had nearly become a savory pastry. Unfortunately, Jammu was not as carefree. He wore his worries like a 100-pound sack of rice. He did what he thought was right, but that did not make him any less hungry. All the rightness in the world did not change the fact that he was a stranger in a strange town, cast adrift and separated from Nana. As a result, Jammu was losing faith in a good and ordered universe. He began to suspect that he could have lived forever, or died today, and the universe would not have cared less.

But contrary to these existential misgivings, the universe did notice Jammu sulking away from the bakery. Or, at the very least, two older boys within the universe did. And they cared very much. As Jammu limped by, the teenagers exchanged a conspiratorial look. Miss Patrice was not the only one who saw a golden opportunity in a crippled boy and his goat.

Jammu did not notice being followed as he roamed the streets of Mbanza. But the two older boys were never far away, lurking and biding their time. Had Jammu known that these sinister shadows were on his trail, he would have stuck to public places and the safety of crowds. But the sun was bearing down, and Jammu wanted to find somewhere cool and quiet to figure out next steps. Oblivious to the danger on his heels, a secluded alley that connected two streets looked like a welcome place to collect his thoughts.

The alley was empty except for a tall stack of crates. As Jammu passed the crates, he saw a large green truck with a canvas back that was not visible from the street. The truck was parked next to an open garage door. Although there were no lights on in the garage, Jammu heard grunts, thuds, and other sounds of heavy lifting inside. Jammu ignored whatever was happening in the garage. He continued deeper into the alley, anxious to have a moment to himself.

But Jammu was not as alone as he supposed. Once he was away from the street, he noticed a noise behind him. The clap of plastic flip-flops echoed ominously off the narrow walls. Jammu turned and saw an older boy standing at the alley entrance. The older boy smiled a wide yellow smile. Jammu suddenly felt very alone.

"Hey, you, kid!" the older boy shouted as he marched towards Jammu. "Where are you from? You don't look like you're from around here. You look lost. I think you need some help."

Jammu did not respond to the older boy. He decided to put as much distance between himself and the street tough as he could. But a boy with one good foot and a goat in tow could only move so fast.

"Where did you get that goat?" the older boy continued. "That goat looks real familiar. I know what it is: that looks just like the goat I lost yesterday. Did you find my goat? Yes, I think you did. Slow down. Let me give you a reward!"

Despite the oppressive heat, Jammu felt a chill ripple through his body. It was like fear had poured a bucket of ice water on his head. Jammu stooped down to pick up his goat and run when a second older boy appeared at the other end of the alley, blocking his escape.

"Hey, kid," the second boy said. "What are you doing with our goat?"

Jammu didn't have time to think before the boys rushed him from both sides. Their flip-flops clip-clopped like a charge of plastic cavalry.

It was not much of a fight: it certainly wasn't a fair one. Jammu lay on the ground half-conscious as the boys tried to search his pockets. But Jammu's pants were shredded during his journey across the savanna, and there were no pockets to search. Offended by this fact, the older boys gave him a parting kick for their trouble. With his cheek against the ground, Jammu watched them drag away his goat.

Jammu wanted to cry after the boys to tell them to stop, but he only managed to drool into the dirt. His tongue was like a dead slug in his mouth. His brain pounded. He couldn't figure out how to stand up, much less fight for his goat. Only God could help Jammu now. And up to that point, God hadn't shown an inclination to positively intervene in his affairs.

But, Jammu's doubts notwithstanding, there was an intervention. As the older boys passed the parked truck, hooting and laughing as they pulled the rope around the goat's neck, something emerged from the garage and grabbed them. Jammu could only make out a blur. But it was a big blur. The size of a rhino. With the speed of a gazelle. And a pair of patched pants that reminded Jammu of giraffe hide. There was a scuffle. Then the sound of choking and voices gasping for air. Jammu tried to focus, but his vision swam and faded. From where he was lying, splayed in the dirt, Jammu could only make out the older boys' legs, which were suspended in the air and being shaken back and forth like the limbs of rag dolls. Their flip-flops flew from their limp feet. The last thing Jammu saw before he passed out was his goat trotting towards him, emerging into focus against the blur of violence.

8

Olson had never been a morning person, but morning in Mbanza was its own special horror. As soon as dawn broke, the heat and humidity soared like a vicious raptor bird. By the time the rooster in the street started to crow, the atmosphere in his room above the Fistula Initiative offices approximated a wet sauna. A metal standing fan rattled at the foot of his bed. The muggy circulation offered little relief and created the unpleasant sensation that an enormous animal was breathing on him. Olson gave up trying to sleep. He slapped away the empty bottle of Tipo Tipico, pushed through the mosquito nets, and faced the rotten day.

He stumbled down the stairs, disheveled and unshaven. Gary was in the kitchen. He was slouched over the table, shoveling cereal into his mouth as he worked out the puzzle on a cornflakes box. Sitting there, contently scrutinizing the cereal packaging, he could have passed for a sweet and slightly-impaired man-child, getting ready for his job cleaning toilets at a gas station. If Olson hadn't known better, he would have never pinned Gary for a trained pilot, who rained fire from above and was responsible for more deaths in Mbanza than dysentery.

Olson tried to reach the coffee without stumbling into a conversation, but Gary, latter-day grim reaper that he was, murdered any hope of that.

"Good morning sunshine," Gary said, his mouth filled with cornflakes.

72

"Nothing good about it," Olson said. He poured the dregs of the coffee pot into his mug. He took a sip and grimaced. It was yesterday's coffee – silty, tepid, and, like Olson, bitter.

"You could make the coffee for once," Olson said. "You know that, right?"

"Do we have to do this every morning?" Gary asked. "Why would I make coffee? I'm Mormon."

It would just be a nice Christian thing to do," Olson said, dumping the coffee down the sink.

"It's not very Christian to a Mormon. You want me to make you coffee? You might as well ask me to slip some whiskey in your cornflakes. It's basically the same for me."

"I wouldn't object to either of those things," Olson said.

Olson took the can of Folgers from the cabinet. He frowned as he dumped the grounds into the coffee maker. It was just his luck. He was on a continent surrounded by great coffee-producing nations. Ethiopia had its Yirgacheffe. Tanzania its Peaberry. Kenya had, well, it made coffee too. But here in Mbanza, Olson could only get Folgers. He didn't understand why Gary bothered about his soul. Olson wasn't afraid of hell. He was already there.

"Sometimes I worry about you," Gary continued. "I don't think Africa agrees with you. It's making you savage."

"Well, at least there is one thing that we can agree on," Olson said.

"Speaking of savage," Gary said. "Did you read about the albino murders?" He nodded toward an open newspaper on the table.

"What about them?"

"They're terrible."

"What do you know?" Olson said, putting away the Folgers can. The coffee maker began to percolate. "That's two things we agree on in one morning. That's a first. But can we hold the albino murders until breakfast. I'd like to return to the subject of your religious objections to coffee."

"Go ahead. Shoot," Gary said.

"You talk about religion all the time, but you have no qualms about flying drones and dropping bombs on people. You're so blood thirsty, you spend your free time gunning people down on your Xbox. You're simulating mass murder. How do you reconcile that?"

"In a couple ways," Gary said. "First, if you want to be technical, I'm not shooting people on the Xbox. I'm shooting aliens."

"That's a distinction without a difference," Olson said. "It's still a bloodbath."

"Second, Joseph Smith never said anything about video games," Gary said. "According to my holy book, I'm good."

"You are a piece of work," Olson said. "Where'd they dig you up again?"

"Reno."

"I thought Mormons were all in Utah."

"We're spreading."

"Like a disease," Olson muttered.

"Or like a healthy, thriving religion," Gary said.

"It's essentially the same thing," Olson said.

The coffee finished brewing. Olson joined Gary at the table, armed with a cup of Folgers that looked and tasted like hot pondwater. Gary had finished decrypting the word puzzle on the cereal box and poured a second bowl of cornflakes.

"You were in late," Gary said.

"I was busy with a bunch of clowns."

"Clowns? Is that some kind of secret agent code I should understand?"

"Nope, I's talking about actual clowns," Olson said.

"What took so long?"

"Have you ever interrogated a mime?" Olson grimaced as he sipped the cup of pondwater. "Never mind. I don't want to get into it. The experience was not nearly as fun as it sounds."

"I don't think that's possible," Gary said. "Clowns are great. I've been crazy about them my whole life. Every time the circus came to town, I made my parents take me. Some kids would go for the elephants. Others would go for the trapeze artists. Not me though. I came for the clowns. I used to watch those clowns pile out of their little clown car and wish they could take me for a ride. I'd even have dreams about it."

"You mean that you had *nightmares*," Olson corrected. "Clowns are terrifying. No one likes clowns. Is every Mormon as weird as you are?"

"At least the ones in Reno," Gary said. "But then again, everyone in Reno is a little off. By the way, if you're going out today, can you grab some milk? We're out."

"Get your own milk," Olson grumbled. "I'm not your delivery service."

The sound of a ringing telephone came from down the hall. It was Olson's cell phone. He remembered that he left the phone in his office when he got back last night.

"Oh, yeah," Gary said, reacting to the ringing as he shoveled a spoon of cornflakes into his mouth. "Your phone has been ringing all morning. It might be important."

"It might be important? You're only telling me this now?" Olson said, getting to his feet. "How long have you been wasting my time, talking about clowns."

"I cherish our conversations," Gary said. "Besides, didn't you tell me to stay out of your business? To stick to the drones? I'm respecting your personal space."

Olson didn't engage with Gary's last remark. He stomped down the hall and slammed his office door behind him. His cellphone was ringing and jittering across his desk. Olson picked up the phone and saw Laurent Congolo's number displayed. There was a dozen missed calls.

Olson flicked the remaining coffee in his mug into the trashcan. Depending on how the conversation went, he wanted to have an empty receptacle for something stronger than weak coffee. The clock on the wall indicated that it was only 8 a.m., but it was never too early to have a drink when the provincial deputy secretary of justice was involved.

Olson raised the phone to his ear and answered the call. A torrent of angry words assailed him. He immediately started searching for a fresh bottle of Tipo Tipico.

"Where are they, Olson? Where are my guns?" the voice in the phone barked.

"And good morning to you, Congolo," Olson replied.

"We had an agreement. The weapons were to be delivered before dawn. But dawn has come and gone. And I have no guns."

"I don't know what you're talking about. I have my best man on it," Olson said, omitting the fact that Kruger was also his only man. "The shipment was loaded and ready for delivery last night. I saw to it myself."

"Well something happened between last night and this morning. I assured my superiors that these guns would be delivered by dawn. You promised me these guns!"

The more Congolo spoke, the more agitated and broken his English became. Despite his knack for languages, Olson struggled to follow the angry word stream gushing from the phone.

"Don't get your panties in a bunch, Congolo," Olson said, trying to shake drops from an empty rum bottle he found on his bookshelf. "What's the big deal? Nothing in this country is ever done on time. If you needed the guns today, you should have asked me to deliver them last week."

"Is this a joke to you?" Congolo snapped. "This is not a joke to me. To my superiors. Or, might I say, to the Mountain Dew Corporation! The MILF continues to threaten their mines. If the yellow dye # 5 supply is interrupted, it will be on my head!"

Olson threw open desk drawers, intensifying his search for that drink. Naturally, Mountain Dew was involved. Big soda's sticky fingerprints were all over it. In Mbanza, it always came back to that damn dye. While Mbanza didn't have much that would feed, enrich, or in any way benefit its population, it had been perversely blessed with the largest naturally-occurring reserves of yellow dye # 5 in the world. These reserves were critical to Mountain Dew's mission to keep soda neon green and teenagers impotent the world over. Olson couldn't imagine a more embarrassing resource curse. He was ashamed to play any part in it. He longed for the old days when wars were fought over diamonds, bauxite, rare earth minerals, and oil. Even bananas were better than this.

"I need those guns," Congolo said. "I don't need to remind you that my position depends on keeping my superiors happy. If Mountain Dew is unhappy, my superiors will be very unhappy. I will be replaced. And if I go, I promise that the next provincial deputy secretary of justice in Mbanza will not be nearly as good a partner to you as I am."

Olson audibly groaned into the phone. As much as he liked the idea of Laurent Congolo disappearing from his life forever, he liked the idea of leaving Mbanza one day even more. As awful as Congolo might be, he was dependably awful. The devil he knew was better than the devil he didn't. With a heavy heart, Olson decided to be accommodating.

"Alright, Congolo. I get it," he said. "I don't know where your shipment is, but I'll find out."

Furious French words still exploded from the phone as Olson hung up. He immediately called Kruger. The call went directly to voicemail. Olson tried again with the same result.

Olson paced around his office. He tried to imagine why Kruger didn't answer. There was no end to the list of things that might have gone wrong. Kruger could have been kidnapped by the MILF, killed by robbers, driven into a mine field, had a flat tire, or been mauled by a lion, which still occurred from time to time. Any awful thing could have happened, but no one scenario was more likely than any other. And for all the unanswered calls, Olson held out hope that Kruger had avoided the worst possibilities. Despite his bargain basement rates, Kruger was capable. He knew his way around chaos and could navigate danger. He came from a long line of gun runners and mercenaries that stretched back to when his melatonin-deficient great-grandfather emigrated from Holland to sun-ravaged Africa. Still, something must have happened. If the Afrikaner was good for anything, it was a constitutional inability to be late. Despite a century of skin damage beneath the equatorial sun, punctuality was encoded in Kruger's protestant genes.

Olson prepared to track down Kruger and the lost shipment. He reached into his desk drawer for a disguise. He selected his bushiest mustache and a big pair of black sun glasses. After he put them on, he looked like the love child of Saddam Hussein and Muammar Gaddafi. Dictatorially-dressed, Olson started down the hall. Gary called to him as he passed the kitchen.

"If you're heading out, can you grab some milk?" he asked, shaking the empty milk carton in the air.

Olson didn't respond. He was already mentally mapping where Kruger might be. He traced the Afrikaner's planned journey from the warehouse to the drop-off location on the outskirts of Mbanza, dropping pins along the route where things could have gone sideways. But just as Olson marched through the reception of the Fistula Initiative and threw open the front door to start his wild geese chase, the search ended. Olson came face to face with Kruger, lurking on the doorstep, alive and in the sunburned flesh. Kruger panted and huffed as he tried to catch his breath. His eye patch was askew and sweat glistened on his soul patch. He looked as though he had just finished a marathon.

If Olson was glad to find Kruger safe, he didn't show it. "What are you doing here?" he muttered, confused and angry. "What happened to the shipment this morning? Where were you? Why didn't you call? And where are my guns?"

Kruger continued to gulp air. "I'm lucky to be here at all," he said between breaths. "I ran into the damn blue helmets!"

"Blue helmets?" Olson asked as he ripped off his fake beard. "You mean the peacekeepers?"

"Yes, I mean the peacekeepers," Kruger said. "They set up a roadblock outside of town. They are stopping every vehicle, checking for contraband. What could I do? The truck was loaded with machine guns. I could not get past the blue helmets. Not with those guns. Not a chance."

As he spoke, Kruger had started swaying from side to side, stepping gingerly from one foot to the other. He pawed unconsciously at his crotch area. "Can I use your toilet?" he blurted out, abruptly interrupting his story.

"No, you can't use my toilet," Olson said. "Not until you tell me what happened to the shipment."

"Like I said, there is a roadblock," Kruger said, grimacing as he restrained his bladder. "The blue helmets were checking everything. So I turned around and drove back up the road, away from town. They shouted for me to stop. When I didn't stop, they started shooting. Fortunately, blue helmets can't shoot straight. Thank god they were from the United Nations. Those blue helmets are more useless than even the African Union peacekeepers. Or even . . ."

"Cut it," Olson snapped, wholly uninterested in the relative capabilities of peacekeeping forces. "Where's the truck? Are the guns alright?"

"The guns are fine," Kruger said. He gestured into the alley where a green truck with a canvas top was parked behind a pile of crates. "But the truck? The truck is not so good."

"You just parked in the alley?" Olson swore, pushing past Kruger.

"What's the big deal? No one can see it from the road. But wait! What about that toilet?" Kruger cried and chased after his employer.

Olson marched to the back of the truck. He threw open the canvas flap, eager to see the guns with his own eyes. But the back of the truck was empty. The guns were gone. In their place, an African boy in rags lay unconscious in the truck bed. A little goat stood over the boy protectively.

The goat bleated at Olson. Olson let the canvas flap fall back down.

"Kruger, where are my guns?" Olson said. His voice was icy. His face twisted like he'd bitten into a bad mussel. "And why is there a boy in the truck?"

"It's a long story," Kruger said, breathing heavily after running after Olson. "You see I saw the boy. . ."

"Kruger. I don't care about the boy."

"But you asked . . . "

Olson took a deep breath, trying to contain his rage. "Kruger, I repeat, where are my guns?"

Kruger adjusted his eye patch and continued his story. "Like I said, they started shooting. I drove away as fast as I could. I'm lucky they didn't hit the guns in the back with all that ammunition. We wouldn't be having this conversation. But they hit something. The truck is making terrible, awful noises."

"I don't care about the truck," Olson said. "I care about the guns. Where are they?"

"I went back to the warehouse. I unloaded them. There was nowhere else to go."

"You went back to the warehouse? Damnit, Kruger. Did they follow you?"

"No, I was not followed," he said, puffing up with offense. "I know this country like the back of my hand. Generations of Krugers have lived in Africa. I'm like a ghost. I disappear into the bush. No one follows me unless I let them."

"Okay, fine, Kruger. You're a great white ninja. You weren't followed. But if there's a roadblock, how did you get the truck back into Mbanza? There is only one road in and out of town, and I'm sure they'd recognize your truck if they had just used it for target practice."

"I pulled off the road and drove cross-country," Kruger said. "Made a big loop around the town and came in the other side. They were watching the road and never saw me."

"If it was that easy to get by them, why didn't you bring the guns when you came back?"

"The ground is too rough. Too much brush. Even without the load of the guns, the truck barely made it." Kruger stroked his soul patch worriedly. "Like I said, there is something wrong with the truck. It may be the transmission. It sounds like someone dies when I change gears."

Olson considered the situation and swore. "The road was clear yesterday," he said. "There were no roadblocks. I checked it myself. We missed the window by a day. How many peacekeepers were at the road block?"

"The blue helmets?" Kruger said. "I don't know. I was trying to escape, not count them."

"Just ballpark it," Olson said.

"Ball? Park?" Kruger asked, unfamiliar with the term, or baseball in general.

"Just guess. Give me a rough estimate," Olson snapped.

"I don't know. Maybe ten," Kruger said with a shrug.

"Ten? Is that all?" Olson shook his head. "You turned around for ten soldiers? Why did you even stop? You could have just driven through them."

"You're paying me to drive a truck. Not run over people. If you want me to drive over people, it costs more." Kruger paused. "By the way, on the subject of payment. . ."

"What about it?" Olson asked.

"When do I get paid?"

"Paid for what?" Olson asked. "Taking a joy ride through the bush? I hired you to deliver guns. As of now, the guns haven't been delivered."

"But I did my part," Kruger said. "I drove the truck. The road block was not my fault."

"Fault has nothing to do with it. You're not paid until Congolo gets his guns," Olson said. "Not until we figure out what to do about those peacekeepers."

"Couldn't you just drop a bomb on them?" Kruger suggested. "You drop bombs on everything else."

Olson considered the suggestion. A drone strike would get rid of the peacekeepers. But the last thing that Olson needed was another international incident after Benghazi. He didn't think that HQ could send him anywhere worse than Mbanza, but he didn't want to give them an excuse to try.

No, drones were no good. The peacekeepers had to leave the road by their own free will. The trick was how to make them do it. What Olson needed was a diversion. Unfortunately, everything remotely diverting in Mbanza had been bombed out years ago. But as Olson considered the situation, inspiration struck. An ember of his old creativity kindled and flared in his brain. For the first time in a long time, he felt the thrill of improvisation.

Kruger had watched the process of inspiration play out on Olson' face. The smile that formed on his employer's lips made him uneasy. Kruger rarely saw Olson smile and, as a result, the muscles were out of practice. The effect was off-putting. Although he couldn't put his finger on it, Olson's expression, which was almost a snarl, seemed crooked, as though deranged or even touched by madness.

"We're looking at this all wrong, my friend," Olson said. "Violence is not the answer. A diversion is in order. We need to give those guards something else to do besides stare at a dirt road. We need to give them somewhere else they want to be."

"Where else would they 'want' to be in Mbanza?" Kruger asked. "This town is a waste. There is nothing here."

I agree. There is nothing here. At least not yet anyway," Olson said. "Kruger, have you ever been to a circus?"

9

Camden, Piper, Jody, and the others were released from the police station the next morning. They descended the hill where the old town sat and wandered the slums on the plain below. They found their way to a rubble field on the outskirts of Mbanza. As the sun climbed higher, the morning heat became oppressive. The group decided to rest and collect themselves after their night in prison.

The rubble field, which was in the process of being reclaimed by weeds and savanna scrub, was empty except for one wall standing by the road. The wall had once been part of a school. The wall, scorched and pocked with bullet holes, was all that remained of that school.

Oblivious to its violent history, Camden squatted behind the ruined wall. His pants were around his ankles and his face was red. For the last twenty minutes, he had tried, and failed, to use the bathroom. During that time, intervals of futile straining and constipated grimaces were interrupted by passing locals. When they appeared, Camden would quickly cinch up his pants and pretend to count the bullet holes in the wall.

Camden should not have bothered being embarrassed. His bare white behind would not have scandalized anyone. Mbanzans were no shrinking African violets. They had survived war, hardship, famine, and death. They had seen much worse than a grown man poo. In fact, public defecation was perfectly acceptable. The plumbing hadn't work in Mbanza years – and there had never been much of it to begin with. Crapping in the streets had become as natural as whistling a tune or saying hello to neighbor. It was not uncommon for some of the more outgoing residents to do all three at once. After experiencing waves of humiliation, however unnecessary and brought upon himself, Camden's Sisyphean shit finally ended when a food distribution truck parked across the street, attracting the better part of the neighborhood. As the crowd swelled around the truck, he hiked up his pants for the last time and gave up any hope of a BM that morning. Camden emerged from behind the wall, bowlegged and walking gingerly. The others were where he'd left them. Despite the heat, they were in fine fettle. With the exception of Camden, no one seemed the least bit bothered about loitering in a weed-choked rubble field in a strange African country.

Lukas was sitting in the dirt, polishing the prop knives and swords that the Mbanzan police had inexplicably let him keep. In accommodation to the climate, he had removed his top hat and lathered his bald scalp with a thick film of sunscreen. Although his vest and utilikilt remained on, Camden confirmed with an unhappy eyeful that Dutchman had dispensed with underwear.

The twins were on the opposite side of the ruined wall where Camden had failed to use the bathroom. They were painting some sort of mural. Where they found the paint and brushes, Camden had no idea. In the center of the mural, there was what appeared to be a pig forcing a topless African woman to eat an apple. Bulgarian scribbles graffitied the background. Camden couldn't read Bulgarian and, as the twins were mimes, there was no point in asking for a translation. But among the Cyrillic word scramble jumble, Camden recognized the word "HIV." The twins were now sketching an aggressively-vascular penis in a perspective that could only be called forced.

Camden quickly lost interest in the mysterious mural. He was focused entirely on Piper. When he had left to use the bathroom, Piper and Jody had been doing some light yoga beneath a balding palm tree. But what began as gentle stretching had evolved into a full-blown exercise in sexy Twister during his absence. Jody lay flat on his back with his feet raised like a pedestal. Piper sat perched on the upraised soles of his feet. With his shapely thighs and thick calves, he launched Piper up and down into the air. Each time Piper took flight, she laughed like a little girl. Each time Piper landed back on Jody's feet, she burrowed her leopard-print bottom into the clutch of Jody's unnaturally prehensile toes.

Camden watched and, despite the blockage in his bowels, felt empty inside. Jody gave Piper a final thrust into the air, launching her higher than before and flipped her forward. Camden gasped, thinking she might land on her head. For a fleeting second, he wondered whether the risk of Piper breaking her neck outweighed the damage such an injury would inflict on her relationship with Jody. But that hypothetical was unanswered. The inversion was part of a routine. As Piper flipped forward, Jody caught her with his feet and held her upside-down by the hips.

"I love being upside down!" Piper exclaimed towards Jody's crotch. "When you're upside-down, the worries fall right out of your head!"

Jody agreed with a hearty laugh and shook her softly with his feet. Piper squirmed and her freckled breasts peeked from her tank top like two furry bunnies emerging from a warren in spring. Jody stopped agitating her and the two locked their eyes. Their breath bated. Piper discretely slid her hands down Jody's thick calves and shapely thighs. The tip of her fingernails probed his shorts.

Before Piper went wrist deep, however, she noticed Camden watching them, staring as stone-faced as an Easter Island statue. His presence ruined the incipient sexcapade. Contradicting her previous assertion about an opposite relationship between inversion and unhappiness, her lips defied gravity to make a frown. She rolled off of Jody's feet with a cartwheel.

"Still at the yoga," Camden muttered as he regained the power of speech. "You seem . . . limber."

"Yoga's about more than stretching," Jody said. He rocked back onto his shoulders and sprung to his feet in a kip-up. "It's a mental attitude. A philosophy. A way of looking at things when they don't go as planned. We're in the wrong country? So what? If you're spiritually flexible, you can make the best of any situation." Jody proceeded to bend backwards into a wheel pose, demonstrating his plasticity in the face of adversity.

"Jody's right," Piper said as she straightened out her tank top. "You need to make it work with what you have. You need to live in the moment."

"Let's live in the moment then," Camden said, unconvinced but in no mood to argue. "What's the plan this moment?"

"That's something we need to decide," Jody said from his backward bridge. "We have to make our own way in this world."

"Okay, then let's make a decision," Camden said. "Let's go home."

"Go home?" Jody scoffed as he returned to a standing position. "We flew forty hours to get here. You just want to go back with your tail between your legs. Is this about last night? That was just a little misunderstanding. You're overreacting, Cammy."

"I came to Africa to perform in a festival. To do a little juggling for a good cause," Camden said. "I'm sorry if spending the night in a police station sucked the adventure out of me."

"You need a thicker skin," Jody said. "This sort of thing happens all the time."

"You spend a lot of time in police stations during vacations?" Camden asked.

Jody frowned and shook his head, as though he was a prophet whose apostle had just failed a trust fall. He addressed his Doubting Camden.

"First, this is not a vacation. This is more important than that. Second, if you don't have run-ins with authority, you're playing it too safe. And what's the big deal anyway? We were already arrested and spent the night in prison. The worst thing that could have happened to us already did. What else is there to worry about?"

"I can think of lots of other 'worst' things," Camden said. "That guy who interrogated us in the jail made it sound like this town is a war zone. We could be robbed. We could be injured. Even murdered."

"Cammy, Cammy, Cammy," Jody said, shutting him down. "That guy in the jail was full of shit. He was trying to scare you. It's standard issue fascist police force tactics. Don't live his lie. Don't let him bring you down."

"He's right, Cammy," Piper added. "You need to relax. Nothing awful happened. We're all fine. It was kind of exciting, right?"

"Exciting is not the word I would use," Camden said.

"Well, no one got hurt. And when this is all over, we'll have a story to tell," she said.

"Piper, I'm good on stories. I have enough stories for one trip. I look forward to telling my grandchildren about the time I spent the night in an African prison."

"You, you, you," Jody said as he retrieved his devil sticks from his bag. He was incapable of standing still. He banged his sticks as he spoke. "Your trip. Your grandchildren. Can you really only think about yourself?"

"Given the present circumstances, I think it's appropriate," Camden said."

"Look around you, Cammy. Look at those people!" Piper said. She gestured to the crowd by the truck across the street where soldiers were distributing bags of rice. "Don't you remember why we came here? It's for those people. We can't let our problems stop us from helping them."

"But we didn't come here to help those people," Camden said. "We came here for the people of Mombasa. Not Mbanza!"

"Semantics, Cammy," Piper said. "The show must go on."

"The show?" Camden was confused. "What show? *Cirque du Poverte* is in a totally different country."

"It's a big continent," Piper said. "There can be more than one show. Jody and I have been talking. Why don't we put on our own show? We're here. We have the talent. And by the looks of those poor people, they could use some joy."

Piper smiled at Camden with excessive hope and gums. But the sentiment was lost on him.

"Piper, seriously, a show is not a good idea. The best thing we can do is go back to the airport and get on the next plane home. We can cut our losses and chalk this up to a life lesson."

Camden thought this was a sensible proposal – perhaps the most sensible thing he'd ever said. But Jody and Piper saw things differently. Piper frowned and shook her head. Jody snatched his devil stick from the air. They looked at Camden as though he admitted to hunting lions or having a sweet spot for shark fin soup.

Jody assumed a paternalistic tone, like the older, wiser brother that Camden had never asked for. "You know, ever since this trip started, I've been watching you," he said. "I've been thinking about you a lot. I've finally figured out what your problem is."

"I didn't know I had one," Camden said.

"Well, you do," Jody said. "And it's that you're too caught up in yourself. You can't see what's really important. But, Cammy, people can change. Even you! Just look at Piper. She had problems when I met her too. She was all bottled up. She was tight like a screw. Now she's like a different woman. She's really blossomed."

"I think Piper was just fine before," Camden said, grating at Jody's insinuations.

"I'm sorry, Cammy. But Jody's right," Piper interrupted. "Before I met him, I was living like I had blinders on. I was sleepwalking. I ate. I slept. I went to class. In my free time, it was just the two of us, watching old movies, going to coffee shops, and putting on our little two-person juggling shows on the quad."

"I liked those juggling shows," Camden said.

"But really, Cammy, what kind of life is that?"

"A nice one?"

"Sure, it was nice," Piper said impatiently. "But it was not an intentional life. Jody showed me that. I can see it now. And you could too, Cammy, if you'd only get out of your comfort zone."

"Comfort zone?" Camden said, choking on the words. "I spent forty hours on planes flying to Africa. I spent the night in jail. And I'm sitting in a rubble field. I promise you that I'm very uncomfortable."

"It's not a question of geography," Jody said. "It's not the number of miles that you fly or where you spent the night. It's about opening yourself up to new experiences. It's about evolving and becoming more human."

"I am a perfectly adequate human," Camden said. "And so is Piper."

"Oh, Cammy. You're sweet," Piper said. "But this is not about us. It's about something bigger. Can't you feel it in the air?"

"You mean the humidity?" Camden asked.

"Not the humidity," Piper said, annoyed. "The energy in the air. It's like a static charge. It's like the universe has something in store for us. It's like we're meant to put on a show. Look! We're already getting an audience!"

Piper pointed to the wall where the Bulgarian twins were just putting the final touches on the mural. Several children had gathered, snickering and pointing, at what was now undoubtedly a penis graffitied on the wall.

"Piper's right," Jody said. "Look how happy we're making these kids. Look at the joy we're bringing. These people deserve a show. They're just dying for it."

Camden agreed that people appeared to be dying of something, but it was not for lack of entertainment. Juggling and acrobatic performances had to be exceedingly low on any Maslow hierarchy of needs.

"This is crazy," Camden said. "How can you talk about putting on a show? We don't even have a stage."

"The world's our stage," Jody said confidently. "We can perform on the street. Who needs a stage when you have talent?"

"This is going to work out!" Piper said and began to hop with excitement. "I can feel it all coming together."

"I can too," Jody said, grabbing her by the forearms. They gazed into each other's eyes. "This is going to happen. The universe is going to make this happen for us."

Camden could not believe what he was hearing. It was lunacy. There was no way a show was happening. In his experience, the universe was not in the habit of arranging performances like an existential LiveNation. Their best option was to collect their things and find a flight back home. He had never been so sure of anything in his life.

But before he could open his mouth and that point, a black SUV rounded the corner and roared up the road. The SUV skidded to a stop next to Cammy, Piper, and Jody. The three stared in dumb surprise as the driver-side door flew open, and the man who interrogated them at the police station emerged.

"I've been looking everywhere for you," Olson said. "You said you guys are some kind of performers? Any interest in putting on a show?"

10

Jammu peeled his eyes apart. He didn't know how long he'd been unconscious. Thoughts came slowly to his bruised brain. The last thing he remembered was lying half-senseless in an alley. He was now sitting upright in a truck, buckled into a seatbelt. The truck was stopped, but the engine was running. It was bright and hot in the cab. The torn plastic seats burned his thighs and sweat pooled on his backside. He had no explanation for what he was doing in the truck or how he'd gotten there. Jammu's sense of dislocation was only alleviated by the sight of his goat sitting between his feet, chewing quietly on a floor mat.

Somewhat reassured, Jammu looked across the dusty bench seat and saw a man wedged behind the steering wheel. He was an enormous man, as stout as an oil drum. His skin was pink with a lifetime of sunburns. His right eye was concealed by an eye patch, his chin by a soul patch. His pants were a Frankenstein patchwork, having been mended and sewn countless times. The driver was a rare specimen, and Jammu gazed at him the way a naturalist would marvel at a white hippo. Jammu might have stared all day, but a rifle barrel poking through the driver's window firmly grabbed his attention. A conversation was in progress between the driver and a soldier holding the rifle. Jammu saw more soldiers with blue helmets circling the truck outside with their weapons drawn. French wasn't Jammu's first language, but it was the language of commerce — and corruption – in that corner of Africa. Even a lowly goatherd knew enough to get by.

"The boy is very sick," the driver was explaining to the rifle barrel. "I must get him to a doctor."

"If you're looking for a doctor, you're going the wrong way," the soldier said with a snarl. Even without the machine gun, he would have been threatening. His face was angry, as hard and black as coal. If not for the baby blue helmet on his head, the solider would have been truly terrifying.

"The town is behind you," the soldier continued. "Where are you going?"

"There is nothing in that town for the boy," the driver growled, indifferent to the rifle barrel in the window. "The doctors in Mbanza are savages. Damn witch doctors. They couldn't tell an aspirin from a bullet in the head. I'm taking him to a real hospital."

Jammu was astonished by the driver's boldness in the face of automatic firepower. But then again, if Jammu was the size of a rhino, he'd be bold too.

"What's wrong with him?" the soldier asked, gesturing towards Jammu.

"Everything is wrong with him," the driver said. "His fever is high, his blood pressure is low, and he hasn't opened his eyes in days. Just look at his foot. It's a horror. He's diseased to the core! If he dies, his blood is on your hands."

The soldier with the blue helmet shrugged. For a peacekeeper, he seemed unperturbed by the prospect of civilian deaths. He took a closer look at Jammu. A thin smile formed on his lips.

"He hasn't opened his eyes in days?" the soldier asked.

"That's right. He could die any minute," the driver said.

"That's funny. His eyes are open now," the soldier said. "He doesn't look so bad to me."

The driver turned and fixed his one good, unpatched eye on Jammu. His pink face flushed to a brighter shade of fuchsia. "It's a miracle," the driver said through gritted teeth. "Don't try to speak, boy. We're going to get you the help you need. Just sit there and keep your mouth shut. Got it?"

Jammu got it indeed. He nodded that he understood.

"Poor thing," the driver said, turning back to the rifle barrel. "He can't speak. Who knows if he'll ever be able to talk again. Now come on, man. Let us go. Don't deny this boy his chance to live."

This appeal did not move the solider. His eyes flicked suspiciously between the driver and Jammu.

"Last night a truck came up the road," the soldier said. "We ordered the truck to stop. When it did not, we opened fire. The truck drove off the road and escaped across the savanna. What do you think about that?"

"I have to admit that it sounds like a reasonable reaction," the driver said. "I'd do the same if you started shooting at me. But other than that, I don't have an opinion."

"Are you sure you don't have anything else to say? It's odd because that truck looked a lot like this truck."

"All trucks must look the same in the dark," the driver said.

The soldier narrowed his eyes. "What were you doing in Mbanza again?"

"I work at a medical charity," the driver said.

"You are a doctor?"

"Do I look like a doctor? Do doctors have pants like these?" the driver grumbled, slapping at his Frankenstein pants. "No, I'm just a driver. I transport things: medicine, supplies, and very sick children."

"And goats too?" the solider said, pointing his rifle barrel at the animal between Jammu's legs.

"The goat is for his family," the driver said. "It's all they own in the world."

"That's a very sad story."

"It's a damn shame."

"What is the name of this charity where you work?"

"It's called the, well . . ." Suddenly, the driver became uneasy. For this first time since Jammu awoke, the man was lost for words. "It's called The Fistula Initiative," the driver said at last. "Their specialty is fistulas."

The soldier with the blue helmet was skeptical. "What is this 'fistula?'" he asked.

The driver cleared his throat and glanced uncertainly at Jammu, as though some knowledge was too heavy a burden for someone so young. He then poked his head out the window and whispered to the soldier. Jammu couldn't hear what the driver said over the rumbling engine. But the words had a striking effect. The color drained from the soldier's face, which paled from dark cacao to a lighter shade of cafe mocha. Without any further questions, the soldier removed his gun from the window. He urged the driver forward as though the truck were loaded with Ebola.

The driver put the truck into gear. The transmission groaned liked a dying animal. The truck pulled away, leaving the peacekeepers and the checkpoint behind.

The driver and Jammu did not speak, but they hardly rode in silence. The engine clanked like a bucket of loose screws. Smoke hissed from beneath the hood as though the truck were powered by steam instead of diesel. As they crawled deeper into the scrubby savanna, the road became more rutted. The bush got bushier. The driver drove with a scowl, regularly craning his neck to look into the side mirror with his good eye. His large hairy knuckles gripped the steering wheel, which looked too small in his hands and liable to break in his grip.

"Where are we going?" Jammu asked, finally working up the courage to speak.

"You do talk," the driver replied without taking his eye off the road. "Don't worry about where we're going. It's not far. I'll let you go when we get there. I don't need you for long."

"Why do you need me at all?" Jammu asked.

"In case we run into more blue helmets. I need the cover. What's an ambulance without a patient? And a crippled boy and his goat are very sympathetic patients. You're my medical passport."

Jammu nodded without understanding. Semi-nomadic goatherders were not familiar with the concept of transit documents.

"I am Jammu," he said.

"I don't care what your name is," the driver said. "But if it makes you feel better, my name is Kruger. Rand Kruger. My friends call me Patches. But I don't have friends. Now that we're familiar, just sit back, shut up, and enjoy the ride."

Jammu tried to do as he was told and enjoy the ride. He really did. He had never ridden in a vehicle, and it was a pleasure to travel across the savanna faster than a limp's pace. But he couldn't stop himself from stealing glances at the large man behind the steering wheel.

Kruger was aware of the attention. He felt Jammu's eyes on him and chafed at the observation.

"Come out with it then," Kruger growled at last. "If you have something to say, say it."

Jammu looked down at his knees as he considered his words. "I want to thank you," he said.

"Thank me for what?" Kruger asked.

"For helping me in the alley. You saved me. And my goat. He is all I have in the world."

Gratitude made Kruger uneasy. "Don't feel too fuzzy about it," he said. "You and that goat mean nothing to me. I just needed the cover. After running into those blue helmets, it's a good thing that I picked you up. But don't start getting ideas. If you don't do as I say, I'll kick you out of this truck. I won't even stop first. I'll just open that door and push. Do you understand?"

Jammu nodded.

Confident that his passenger didn't feel too good about himself, Kruger relaxed. As the truck clunked along, he even chanced some conversation.

"What were you doing in a place like Mbanza?" Kruger asked.

"I was travelling to Unubi," Jammu said. "It's the village that I come from."

"Unubi? I've never heard of it."

"It's only a small village. It's very humble."

"If it's only a small, humble village, why go back?"

"Because the most beautiful girl in the world lives there," Jammu said.

"I doubt that's true," Kruger said. "If the most beautiful girl in the world lives there, I'd have heard about it." While he drove, he began to grimace and shift uncomfortably in his seat.

"But it's true," Jammu insisted. "Her name is Nana. I am going home to marry her. That is why I am so glad that you saved my goat. I need it for the bride price."

"Just one goat, huh? If you can marry a woman for one goat, she can't be that pretty," Kruger said and scratched at his crotch.

Jammu frowned and rubbed his knees. "I had more goats before," he said. "But they are gone now. This one is all I have left. I know he is not enough for Nana. She is worth more than all the goats in the world. But I have no time to get more. Her family wants her to marry the village elder, Teacher Mapouro. I must return soon and stop the marriage."

As Jammu related his romantic woes, Kruger slammed on the brakes and stopped the truck. "Hold that thought," he said. With the engine still running, Kruger hopped out of the truck. He unzipped his pants and started to urinate. He urinated for a long time.

"What were you saying again?" Kruger asked with great relief after he climbed back into the truck.

"I told you about Nana. How she would marry Teacher Mapouro if I didn't return to stop it."

"Yes, that's right," Kruger said as he tortured the transmission into first gear. "This Mapouro. Is he very old?"

"Yes," Jammu said. "He is one of the oldest men in the village."

"And is he ugly?"

"He is as ugly as he is old."

"And I suppose he's very rich too?"

"He is the richest man in the village," Jammu confirmed. "He has chickens, goats, cows, and cassava fields. He even has a satellite on the roof of his house. They say he gets 200 channels."

Kruger nodded, not entirely without sympathy. "That's a tough story," he said. "But if you want my advice, forget about her. A boy like you can't compete with a man like that. Men talk about love. But for women, it's all about the livestock. You're better off alone. Women only complicate things."

"But I love Nana. I can't imagine life without her!" Jammu said.

"I'm sure you do," Kruger said. "You're young. A romantic. I was young once too. I loved a woman. I couldn't imagine life without her. But in the end, I wound up with a broken heart and the clap. Do you know what chlamydia is, Jammu?"

Jammu did not.

"Lucky you," Kruger said and pawed at his crotch. "Stay that way. It's funny. A man can buy may things in this place. AK-47s, RPGs, anti-personnel mines . . . But there isn't a dose of amoxycillin in the whole damn country."

Kruger laughed bitterly. "You are a nice boy. But take my word for it. If you want a woman, love won't do the trick. And neither will that goat. Women only care about two things: power and money. If you want a woman, you need one or the other. Or ideally both. And don't let anybody tell you otherwise."

Jammu sat in silence. Kruger had given him much to consider. After they drove a little farther, Kruger stopped the truck.

"This is as far as you go. Time to get out," he said.

Jammu climbed down from the truck. He separated the goat from the half-eaten floor mat and placed the goat on the ground beside him. Jammu looked around. They were in the middle of the savanna. In the middle of nowhere.

"Mbanza is back the way you came. Stay on the road, you won't get lost," Kruger said. He reached into a cooler by the seat and removed a beer from the now tepid water. "This is so you won't die of thirst," he said, tossing the warm bottle to Jammu.

Without a further goodbye, Kruger pulled the passenger door shut. The truck crawled forward, straining like a man with kidney stones, and turned down a dirt track that branched from the main road. The engine gave off little puffs of smoke as it disappeared into the bush.

Jammu looked at the bottle in his hand. When the cap failed to twist off, he pried it loose with his two front teeth. The cap fell to the road, where the little goat promptly snatched it up and chomped it like aluminum chewing gum. Jammu took a long swig of beer before starting back towards the dot on the horizon that was Mbanza.

11

Olson wouldn't have believed it if he hadn't see it with his own eyes. But there it was. Where there had once been a field of rubble, there was now a circus tent. A sort of big top on the savanna. During his time in Mbanza, he'd witnessed much destruction. But he'd never seen anything built. This was truly a banner day.

Olson peeked inside the tent flap at the entrance. It was by no means pretty. Barnum and Bailey would have rolled over their graves at the sight of it. The peak of the tent was supported by a creosote shell of a dead electricity pole. The tent itself was stitched together from used quarantine tents, which explained the subtle whiff of plague. No, the tent would not have passed muster at even a third-rate, hayseed fair. But for a hastily devised diversion, it worked.

The tent had gone up in only three days. Olson had never imagined that the people of Mbanza could be so productive. This wasn't a broad judgment on Africa. It was a narrow assessment focused on one miserable town. If anyone in the world was justified to drag ass in despair, it was the citizens of Mbanza. And even they were still capable of accomplishments, provided the proper motivation was applied. In this case, the proper motivation was armed soldiers overseeing the construction. It was no spontaneous expression of civic renewal, but after years of famine and war, just finding the wherewithal to get out of bed and be frog-marched to forced labor was some kind of testament to the human spirit.

Olson was still trying to figure out whether he should be inspired or depressed when a dusty BMW came up the road. Laurent Congolo and two guards exited the vehicle. Congolo's arrival pushed Olson's emotional scales decisively towards depression.

"Yes, yes, yes," Congolo said as he approached the tent. He kicked tent stakes, opened and closed the tent flap, and tugged at one of the guide ropes. The rope snapped back from his grip. Its tautness pleased him. He smiled widely as he approached Olson. "Very good. Our little project is coming along nicely. Wouldn't you agree?"

"Sure," Olson said. "Six thousand years of recorded human civilization and your people have mastered the tent. You should be very proud. I think you're ready to finally tackle the wheel."

"You are making a joke," Congolo said. "But I see nothing to laugh about. Three days ago there was nothing here. Now we have a circus. It's a great accomplishment."

"I don't know how 'great' the accomplishment is. But I had my doubts you could pull it off."

"Never underestimate the resourcefulness of the African people. Don't you know that we Africans are great builders? Perhaps the greatest in history. When your ancestors were still living in caves, we build wonders. Have you happened to hear of the pyramids?" Congolo said with oversized pride, as though he had polished the stones himself.

"Pyramids? Africans did that? I thought it was the aliens," Olson said.

"What about the Great Library of Alexandria?" Congolo asked. "The greatest library in the ancient world. Africans built it."

"Maybe Africans built it, but I think Greeks put the books in it."

Congolo narrowed his eyes like an aggrieved serpent. "Your words hurt me," he said. "How dare you mock my people? Have you forgotten about Great Zimbabwe? The glories of Timbuktu? Can you joke about that?"

"Well, you have me there," Olson said. "Timbuktu is a fine piece of work."

"I'm glad that some things are sacred," Congolo said. "Your mockery debases us both."

"Oh, come off it, Congolo," Olson said. "Don't be so damn sensitive. I can't be that bad if we're doing business. You're taking my guns after all."

Congolo threw up his hands in a gesture of helplessness. "What choice do I have? I do what I must. Unfortunately, in my nation's struggle for survival against the MILF, I must work with unfortunate allies. The things one does for one's country."

"You're preaching to the choir," Olson said.

Congolo smiled at the remark. If they could agree on nothing else, it was their mutual disdain.

"Walk with me," Congolo said. "Let's discuss our plan in the shade. You skin is not made for the African sun. You're pinking like a pig."

Congolo led Olson across the street to the latticed shade of a balding palm tree. His guards stood at a respectable distance, watching the street.

"We have done our part," Congolo said, nodding toward the tent. "Construction is almost complete. It will be ready by tonight. Will the performers be ready?"

"They'll be ready. I imagine they're getting into costume as we speak."

"When do we get the guns?" Congolo asked.

"As soon as the peacekeepers are off the road and in that tent, my man will deliver them to your doorstep. With a bow on top."

"And you're sure the peacekeepers will come?" Congolo asked.

"What else do they have to do? They've been sitting on that road watching their fingernails grow for days. I'm sure they're dying for something else to do. But they're not going to come for an empty tent. They need something to guard. A crowd to control. You can supply that crowd?"

"You will have your crowd," Congolo said. "I can assure you the whole town will attend."

"You have enough goons for that?" Olson asked.

"Goons," Congolo gasped, feigning shock. "We don't need goons. The government is benevolent. We have more subtle ways of encouraging behavior than using force."

"How do you plan to manage it then?" Olson asked. "I've seen the rehearsals? This show won't sell itself."

"It's simple," Congolo said. "I stopped distributing aid from food trucks three days ago. We have spread the word that food will be distributed from the tent. The people will come running."

"You've been starving them?" Olson asked. "I'm sure they'll be a lovely audience."

"Yes, they'll be very eager to attend. You will have your crowd," Congolo said. "But still, this subterfuge, this tent. It's a lot of work to distract what, a dozen guards? Isn't it excessive? Couldn't you have just dropped a bomb on them? It would have been much easier."

"What is wrong with all of you people?" Olson asked. "Why does everyone in this country think a bomb is the answer to every question."

"That is a funny thing to hear from the man whose country makes the bombs," Congolo said.

"Enough with the bombs," Olson said. "No bombs. We have the tent. We have the show. And we'll have the audience. Once I get the guards off the road, you'll get your guns. Everybody wins and no one blows up."

"Happy endings for all," Congolo said. "Yes, I can see how it will all work. There is only one thing that would make it better."

"And what's that?" Olson asked.

"A tank," he said.

"You're not getting the tank, Congolo. You're getting guns as agreed. That's the deal. And, honestly, what would you even do with a tank? What's left to blow up in this town?"

"Oh, I can imagine things to do with a tank," Congolo said dreamily. His gaze travelled far away, as though he spied something bright and beautiful on the dirty brown horizon. His eyes shined with hope and power. "We would set it up in the town square. For the glory of Mbanza. It would strike fear into the hearts of the MILF. For miles and miles, the word would spread among our enemies: fear Mbanza, for they have a tank! People would come to marvel at it. Perhaps we could decorate it on holidays."

Then, as if the dream faded and flickered, Congolo's gaze returned to the foreground. He cleared his throat and composed himself. "That is what I would do with a tank."

Olson stared in disbelief. "You're insane, you know that? This country is run by a bunch of clowns."

Congolo shrugged and smiled his thin reptile smile. "We may be clowns. But thanks to you, we are clowns with guns. And guns make a great difference."

While they had been speaking, the streets had filled with gaunt Mbanzans walking towards the tent, traveling for what they thought was a free dinner. But there was now a new element. Among the townspeople was a column of blue helmets, marching in a row.

"Will you look at that. Peacekeepers," Olson said. "I told you'd they'd come."

"So you did," Congolo said distractedly. He looked warily at the Mbanzans coming up the street. The crowd made him uneasy. "If there is nothing else, I think I should be going," he said.

"You aren't staying for the show?" Olson asked.

"No, I am afraid not," Congolo said.

"But they're your people," Olson said. "Don't you want to join them in the tent? You could all watch the show together."

Congolo scowled as though Olson suggested he climb into a bathtub of used water. "Power should retain a respectable distance from the people," he said. "And in any case, my superiors are eager to confirm the shipment. I must inform them as soon as the guns arrive."

With that, Congolo, flanked by his guards, retreated to the BMW and drove away.

Glancing at the sun through the palm leaves, Olson wiped sweat from his brow and planned his own escape to somewhere with more shade and, ideally, a well-stocked bar. Before he could act on this plan, however, his cell phone rang. He fished his phone out of his pocket. It was Kruger.

"You had better be calling to tell me the truck is loaded and you're enjoying the drive back to Mbanza, Kruger."

"Not exactly," Kruger said, his husky voice hedging. "It's the truck."

"What about the truck?" Olson asked.

"The truck is loaded. But the engine sounds like a dying animal. And there is smoke. So much smoke. I don't think the truck will make the drive to Mbanza."

Olson could tolerate no more complication. This mission had been giving him an ulcer for days. Given his routine alcohol intake, it would be a lie to say that it was driving him to drink. But it was no overstatement to say that the mission had, metaphorically-speaking, pulled around the car and handed him the keys.

"I'm not hearing any of this, Kruger," he said. "I am watching the peacekeepers walk into the tent right now. The road is clear. This is our chance. You need to move those guns. I don't care how you do it. Carry them on your back if you have to. But if you want to get paid, you are delivering that shipment tonight."

"But the truck . . ." Kruger protested.

"I repeat, Kruger, I don't care how you do it. Just do it!"

Olson ended the call and shoved the phone back into his pocket. He muttered under his breath and started to head back to the office to kick off a private happy hour when he heard his name.

Olson turned and was shocked to see Gary. He had known the man for six months and not once had he seen him outside of the Fistula Initiative. Gary wore a thick pair of sunglasses and a broad straw hat to shield himself from the sun. Despite these precautions, he was the color of a strawberry and bore an uncanny resemblance to Marlon Brando in *The Island of Dr. Moreau*.

"I don't think I've ever seen you outside," Olson said in disbelief. "I was pretty sure that you were a vampire."

"You always tell me that I should leave the office," Gary said. "When you mentioned there would be a circus, I figured this was my chance."

"Don't tell me you came out just for the show."

"Why not? I'm a big fan of the circus. Do you think there will be clowns?"

"If nothing else, I can promise you'll see some clowns," Olson said. "But don't get too excited. I've seen the rehearsals. It's not the greatest show on Earth. It might actually be the worst."

"I take it you won't be attending?"

"No, I'm not," Olson said. "A clown touched me once when I was little."

"That must have been very painful," Gary said. "If you ever need to talk, let me know. In the meantime, I'll save you some peanuts."

"I don't think they're going to have concessions," Olson said, recalling Congolo's strategic starvation initiative.

"That's alright. I brought my own." Gary lifted a brown paper bag in his right hand and removed a nut. He popped the nut in his mouth and chewed happily.

Olson quickly pushed Gary's hand down and out of sight. "If I were you, I'd keep those hidden," he said gravely. "People have been killed for less."

"What's the big deal?" Gary asked, chomping obliviously. "They're just peanuts."

"Trust me on this one. The natives are peckish. If they smell as much as popcorn on your breath, they'll tear you apart like cotton candy."

Gary nodded uncertainly as he digested the snack food metaphor. He wondered if Olson had already started drinking. "Well, umm, thanks for the warning," he said. He squinted up at the sun. "I better get inside before I melt out here. I want to be sure I get a good spot."

Olson watched Gary disappear beneath the big top. He was ready to call it a day too. The tent was up. The peacekeepers had left the roadblock. And the show would soon start. There was nothing left to do except go back to the office, pour a glass of rum, and wait for good news.

But as Olson headed towards his parked SUV, there was a commotion in the road. A group of Africans trudging towards the tent cleaved in two, jumping to the side as a horrific blur ran between their legs, screeching and spraying blood.

Olson had no idea what he was looking at first. But as the blur came closer, he realized that it was a chicken. A rooster to be exact. The rooster was running for its life. As it approached, Olson got a good look at it. The bird was missing most of its feathers and nearly bald. It was also missing its beak, which explained the blood and the ungodly noise it made. But before the rooster reached him, it wobbled, lost its footing, and collapsed on the road. As it exhaled its last breath, blood bubbled from the face hole and burst, misting the dirt road red.

Olson looked down at the foul carnage at his feet. He was shocked, sickened, and deeply depressed. Moments later, a group of boys broke through the crowd, ran over, and snatched the rooster from the road. That chicken had survived so long only to end up in a cookpot. The boys lifted the rooster triumphantly, like a medieval infantry hoisting and parading a fallen king, as they retreated with their prize.

Olson watched them depart with vague unease. He was not a superstitious man, but a mutilated rooster was not the best omen.

12

Somber and constipated, Camden prepared for the show. He was "backstage," behind the ruined school wall in the rubble field that had been incorporated into the circus tent's construction. This was the same wall upon which the Bulgarian twins had painted their mural days before. Despite coats of light green paint, the mural, in all of its aggressively vascular glory, shown through, revealed like a palimpsest by the bright stage lighting.

In happier times, the process of transforming from dull daytime Camden to a flamboyant and colorful clown was pure pleasure. He once relished the feeling of cool makeup against his skin, the smoothness of his cotton overalls, and the adrenaline that percolated before a performance. But this joy was gone. He straightened his fuzzy green wig and felt nothing.

"I can't find my balls," Camden muttered as he stomped around in a pair of oversized red clown shoes. "Where are my balls?!"

He had searched everywhere. He was sure that he had brought the juggling balls, along with his costume, from the little shack where Olson had arranged for them to stay. They may have fallen out of his bag, but it was too dark to see. He became impatient and flustered. His clown shoes slapped furiously on the dirt floor as he stomped around the backstage in his search. He could have used some help. But despite the scene he made, no one paid him any mind.

"It's a full house!" Piper exclaimed from her position at the wall. Her ginger head disappeared around the corner of the wall and reappeared. "They're pouring in!"

"We know that already," Camden said, bent over with his hands on his knees, scanning the floor. "You've already told us twice."

Piper continued to beam, undeterred by Camden. "I may have said it twice, but it's worth repeating. The tent is packed. The whole town must be in there. And they just keep coming!"

The news rallied the others. Lukas removed a dagger from his throat and cheered. The Bulgarian twins were also apparently pleased. They smiled beneath their white mime makeup and made jazz hands. Once again, Camden was the odd-man out. A lonely Eeyore in the wilderness.

The last few days had been hard on Camden. The only food that he'd eaten was rice with peanut powder and puny round pieces of fruit that were somehow both rotten and not yet ripe. They might have been apples, but since they were inedible, it was impossible to be sure. This fiber-less diet had done no favors for his regularity. But the worst of it, far worse than the malnutrition and constipation, were Piper and Jody.

While planning the show, Piper and Jody had practiced their routine constantly. And with constant practice, the routine became unbearable. They'd become less two individuals than a single, sweaty tantric pretzel. Five minutes did not pass without their genitals being pressed together through the thinnest layer of nylon. It was simulated sex under the pretext of planking. It was downward doggy-style. Every day they rubbed Camden's face in it, and night brought no relief. Once they returned to the little shack, Jody and Piper dropped the non-sexual pretense and engaged in the genuine article. While Camden lay in one room with Lukas and the twins, Jody and Piper took the other. A paper-thin wall left nothing to Camden's overheated and sleepless imagination. He lay prone on the floor, trying to ignore the huffing, grunts, and creaking cot, waiting for morning to come. The morning never came soon enough.

Camden gave up trying to find his juggling balls. He didn't care if he performed. The others were more than ready to pick up the slack. He looked at Piper, bouncing up and down at the edge of the stage. Wearing a spangled crop top that exposed her mid-riff and her leopard print tights, she was dressed to dazzle.

While she peeked out at the crowd, she unconsciously (or, perhaps, not so unconsciously), extended back her leg in an arabesque, throwing the contours of her perky bottom into a distracting relief.

Jody joined the others backstage, swaggering with his devil sticks like some kind of hippie paladin. His outfit was the mirror of Piper's – black tights and a mesh leopard print jersey shirt that would have made a callboy blush.

"I forgot my devil sticks. You never know when these come in handy," he said, waving them in the air. "Holy shit, have you seen that audience? Someone call the fire marshal. We have to be breaking a building code."

"Isn't it great!" Piper agreed as she ran over to Jody. "It's crazy. When we planned this trip, I thought that we were just going to be part of the show. And now we're the headliners. We are the show!"

"I saw some guys with guns and blue helmets making a line in the front of the stage. We're so popular we need security," Jody said. "The news about *Cirque du Poverte, Part Deux* has spread far and wide. We're really going to get our message out."

"And what message is that exactly?" Camden interrupted with a pout. "I thought we just came to put some smiles on faces. I didn't know we had a message."

"Maybe you just came here to make people laugh," Jody said. "But the rest of us have bigger goals. Hey, what's with the long face anyway?"

"It's called makeup," Camden said. "I'm a clown."

"It's not just the makeup. It's something else. What crawled up your butt now? We have a stage. We have our audience. And we're going to put on a show. Show a little excitement. Isn't this why we came to Africa?"

Camden did not respond. He declined to expound on why he came to Africa.

"Cammy's fine," Piper said. "He's just grouchy because he can't find his juggling balls. He's worried that he won't be able to go on."

"You have to go on," Jody said. "But you're the warm-up man. You need to get out there and kick things off."

"I can't juggle without juggling balls," Camden said. "What am I supposed to do, just stand there?"

"You're a clown. Can't you do a magic trick or something?" Jody asked.

"I'm not that kind of clown."

"Well, this is a pickle," Jody said. "Wait I know. He went over to a table where the remains of their late lunch sat. He picked up three of the uneaten "apples." "Juggle with these," he said. "They have to be good for something."

Jody tossed the three apples to Camden. Not expecting them, Camden flailed and ham-fisted the catch. The fruit scattered across the backstage area.

"Maybe you should try to warm up a little?" Piper said uncertainly.

"Yeah, maybe we should change the lineup and give Cammy a chance to practice," Jody said. "Let's have the twins go on first, then Lukas, and then Cammy can come on."

"What about us then?" Piper asked. "When do we go on?"

"We're saving the best for last, babe," Jody said with a wink. He grabbed her by the waist and started to shake.

"This is happening." Piper cried out as she jittered. "Holy shit, this is happening!"

"Did you ever have any doubt?" Jody said.

"Never," Piper said breathlessly.

"Me neither," Jody said, his voice getting husky with libido. "We are doing important work. And when you do important work, the universe finds a way to make things happen. You did this Piper. You made this happen. You're a star. This is your night to shine!"

Camden tried to ignore them as he crawled on his knees, gathering the scattered apples. He looked miserable in a way that went far deeper than clown makeup.

*   *   *

For lack of anything better to do, Jammu joined the crowd moving through the street. Since limping back to Mbanza after his one-way joyride with Kruger, he had spent the better part of three days trying, and mostly failing, to finding something to eat. The town was like an empty cupboard with hardly a crumb to be found. Nothing was available for any price, not that Jammu would have a penny to pay for it. On the rare occasion that he did stumble across something – a brown banana in the road; a bruised apple falling from an overturned crate – he still had no luck. His goat inevitably beat him to whatever morsels they found. This competition for resources was hardly fair considering the goat had four good legs and Jammu only one. As he watched the goat slurp back the banana or overtake the rolling apple, Jammu wrestled with the urge to break one of the animal's legs to level the playing field. He couldn't bring himself to hobble his only friend in the world though, even if that friend was selfish and refused to share.

With an empty stomach and a heavy heart, Jammu dragged his goat along with the crowd. The townspeople looked miserable, half-starved and staggered. Jammu was miserable too and he thought some company might be nice. He regretted his decision to join the procession almost immediately. The arrival of the goat sent an unsettled ripple through the crowd. To Jammu, the shaggy little animal was a friend, not food. Others, however, did not share this sentimental attachment. The goat was the closest thing they'd seen to a meal in days. Famished eyes fixed on the goat and the crowd gathered closer. Jammu tried to ignore the ravenous stares. He held the rope around the goat's neck tighter and prayed that no one tried anything. He was under no illusions that he would be an obstacle if they did.

Fortunately, before things came to a head, word spread that took goat off the menu for the time being. There were whispers among the townspeople that they were headed for food: the government was distributing rations again! With dinner in the immediate offing, consuming Jammu's goat became less a priority, especially considering how long it generally takes to cook a goat and the slightness of the particular goat in question.

Insofar as malnutrition allowed, the crowd picked up the pace. As they marched forward, the speculations about the meal awaiting them swirled and elaborated. Initially, it was just a matter of the usual rice rations. But there was soon talk of bread, fruit, and even meat. The crowd imagined a veritable cornucopia. Jammu heard mention of something called a "buffet," which sounded both delicious and very classy. By the time they reached the edge of the slum, the entire town had joined the crowd. A huge tent awaited them there. A tent flap was open.

The townspeople rushed to enter. Bodies converged, packed shoulder-to-shoulder, and shoved towards the entrance. A head shorter than the crowd and with only one good foot, Jammu was swept along with them. He was carried towards the tent, propelled forward by a kind of peristalsis, as though the starving crowd had metamorphized into one massive intestine that was slowly digesting him. Jammu could not see where he was going. He could barely breathe in the crush. All he could do was hold tight to the rope around his goat's neck. Just when he thought he might suffocate, the pressure eased. He passed through the pinch-point at the tent flap and stumbled forward into the open tent.

Free from the crowd, Jammu got his bearings. The tent was only half full but filling fast. It was dark inside the tent. Strings of dim lights were strung from an old electricity pole that supported the structure. Jammu peered through the gloom in search of the meal that was promised. But after a cursory inspection, he saw no sign of food. Based on the swearing and muttering around him, others had the same observation. They didn't know why they were there, but it was certainly not for a buffet.

As far as Jammu could tell, all of Mbanza was packed into the tent. He had arrived in town less than a week prior, but he recognized many faces. There was the yellow-eyed porter from the Hotel Internationale who had chased him with the broom. Despite the stifling heat beneath the canvas big top, he still wore his starched wool bellhop uniform. Miss Patrice, of savory pie fame, was there too. After three days without any filling for her pies, the large woman was noticeably reduced, shrunken like an overripe banana that couldn't fill its withered skin. Jammu wandered to the far end of the tent and found a makeshift stage assembled from wooden crates in front of an off-white brick wall. A line of soldiers with blue helmets and automatic weapons formed a protective ring around the stage. Among the blue helmets was the soldier with the fearsome gaze that had stopped Kruger at the checkpoint. Jammu didn't wait to find out if the solider remembered him. He retreated with his goat to a dark corner.

Jammu was so disappointed that the promised buffet had not materialized that it was some time before he realized that he was not sulking in the shadows alone. He startled when he perceived a man in the darkness. But his stunned surprise was replaced by a more enduring interest. First, unlike everyone else in the tent, the man was white. Second, also unlike everyone else in the tent, the man was conspicuously well-fed. These two facts alone were grounds for mild curiosity. But the man became absolutely fascinating when he removed a peanut from a paper bag, discretely cracked the shell, and tossed the nut into his mouth.

Gary did not fail to notice Jammu's slack jaw stare or outstretched palm reflexively seeking a handout. It could have been an awkward moment, a metaphor for global inequality represented by a westerner with many nuts and a malnourished boy with none. Although his job was dropping bombs on strangers, Gary was a bridge-builder and had a large heart to match his waistline. He offered a kind word in English. When this word generated no response, Gary kindly offered his paper bag and shook a few peanuts into Jammu's open hand.

For a brief moment, Jammu gawked at the peanuts in his grasp, as though they had appeared by magic. But he quickly overcame his enchantment and slammed the nuts into his mouth, shells and all.

Jammu was still probing his teeth for flecks of peanut when light filled the tent. A childish smile spread across Gary's face as he looked across the crowd. Along with the rest of the assembled citizens of Mbanza, Jammu turned towards the front of the tent where, beyond the phalanx of blue helmets, a figure appeared on the makeshift wooden stage.

*   *   *

Lukas emerged from the darkness and walked across the stage of crates. He stepped lightly. The splintered planks creaked as though they might collapse at any moment. But despite the stage's questionable integrity, he was all excitement, beaming a broad, if blind, smile into a pair of klieg lights that had been deployed for the performance. Dressed to the sword-swallowing nines, Lukas wore his finest kilt. Affixed to a belt with an enormous steel buckle were more blades that a *Ginsu* knife infomercial. His top hat and vest (*sans* undershirt) added a touch of class. Upon reaching the stage's apron, he removed his hat with a flourish and bowed, exposing his bald head to the crowd. Returning his hat to his head, he stood with arms akimbo and thrust out his hips, revealing to the front row what was beneath his kilt.

Lukas looked proudly out onto the assembled crowd. The crowd looked back with limited patience. The townspeople had come to the tent for food, not this tall, pale, and underwearless man. Despite the palpable restlessness in the tent, Lukas began to hype the show, announcing in English that they were the lucky audience of something called *Cirque Du Poverte, Part Deux*. The crowd offered little response, and none of it was positive. Of course, the audience spoke no English. But even if they had, anything but clear and concise directions to food would be cause for outrage.

As Lukas spoke, the crowd became increasingly testy. What began as a murmur of discontent started to seethe and simmer. The crowd pulsed and pressed against the peacekeepers guarding the stage. The crowd started to hurl insults. Then they started to throw things. After an airborne sandal assassinated his top hat, Lukas decided that the audience was sufficiently hyped. He cut the speech short and transitioned to his act. He pulled a knife from his belt and presented it to the crowd. The sight of the knife threw the crowd into a fit. Assuming the blade was some sort of insult or provocation, the audience surged against the line of blue helmets, who beat them back with a liberal application of rifle butts. The atmosphere in the tent was getting truly nasty when Lukas did something no one saw coming. After he wet the blade, licking it like a chrome lollipop, he raised the knife in the air and plunged it down his throat.

The audience went silent. When the knife made its appearance, no one had expected Lukas to use his neck as a sheath. But even more surprising than that was the fact that he was not dead. On the contrary, the strange pale man was still on his feet and exhorting to the crowd for applause with his arms. Unfortunately, the crowd was too traumatized to oblige. When Lukas extended his arms, bent at the waist, and grinned with his teeth against the hilt, the audience let out a communal gasp.

Lukas repeated the sword-swallowing trick several times with the assorted cutlery in his belt. The crowd watched in astonished horror. His consumption of a miniature curved scimitar, which required him to bend sideways to accommodate the blade, made a particular impact.

After the initial shock passed, the audience began to grasp for explanations. No one in Mbanza had ever seen or heard of a sword swallower. Out of the whispers, the initial consensus was that the knives were fake. But a complicated theory premised on illusion was quickly replaced by a simpler hypothesis: the crowd was witnessing magic, and the strange man on the stage was a wizard. With three days of hunger feeding their calorie-deprived imaginations, the idea resonated.

Fear, anger, and superstition coursed through the tent. Unable to read the room for the klieg lights in his eyes, Lukas mistook the chaos for a vigorous

113

ovation. The rest of the troupe backstage, unable to clearly see the crowd, reached a similar erroneous conclusion. Before Lukas had finished tasting the blades in his belt, the second act made a premature appearance as the Bulgarian twins rushed out from the wings. Dressed in black leotards and with mime white faces, the twins fluttered across the wood crates, doing their best impersonation of mute birds. With each exaggerated step, their knees touched their chests like storks striding through shallow water. They beat their arms like wings. Their hair was teased into nest-like messes for artistic measure.

The Mbanzans in the tent didn't pay much consideration to the avian quality of the twins' performance. But the twins' preternaturally white skin caused an immediate stir. Ominous sub-currents rumbled through the crowd. Cries of "albinos" erupted like geysers from the audience, joining a chorus of words that included "wizard," "rice," and "buffet."

The audience worked itself into a fine froth. The blue helmets trying to keep order were overwhelmed and driven back against the stage. It was into this chaos that Camden stumbled with a big green wig, bigger red clown shoes, and three apples for juggling. He had been urged – or more accurately "pushed" – onto stage by Piper who was eager for her chance to bask in what she thought was riotous applause as compared to, well, an actual riot.

Camden blocked the stage lights with his hand and peered into the dark tent. He did not like what he saw. Lukas, who had happily turned to the fire-breathing portion of the routine, was applying paraffin to a torch. The twins continued to scamper from one end of the stage to the other. Only Camden was aware of the rage coursing through the crowd like distemper in a wild dog. His makeup was streaked with fear and constipation. He resembled a pad of melting butter.

If Camden had been slightly less panicked, he probably would have turned and ran. But the extremis of the situation overpowered his senses. His rational responses failing, Camden's mind grasped at the comfort of habit. Unsure of what else to do, he lifted his apples and started to juggle. With the appearance of the apples, the fury in the crowd entered a new gear. It was not enough that they had been starved, deprived, and lured to a tent under false pretenses. Now they had to endure a green-haired man mock them with the first food they had seen in days.

Camden tried to go through his routine, but the hostile crowd knocked him off his game. If he could have made it through his progression, he might have gotten off the stage before any real trouble erupted. But Camden was not so lucky. His nerves were frayed. He started to shake. He started to tremble. His hands became two wet clams, and the apples slipped from his bivalve grip. As he transitioned from his three-ball-cascade to a waterfall, the apples tumbled down and rolled across the stage.

The front row of the audience lunged at the fruit, pinning the peacekeepers against the stage. Camden instinctively chased the apples to the apron. The crowd snatched two before he could reach them. Camden managed to get his fingers on the third, just as a hand from the crowd reached out and grabbed it. The crowd went apoplectic as Camden engaged in an ill-advised tug-of-war for the bruised fruit. Enraged, the audience swelled forward. The thin line of blue helmets crumpled and disappeared beneath the crowd.

Giving up on the apple, Camden fled as the crowd swarmed the stage. The others, however, were not as alive to the imminent threat. The twins were still skipping and flapping their arms as the crowd – which had now graduated to a proper mob – encircled. The twins only noticed the crowd at the last minute. Their eyes opened wide and their mouths made terrified "o's." As the mob converged, they held out their palms pathetically, as though there was an invisible wall to protect them. Mimes to the last, they didn't make a sound as the crowd bore down.

As he ran toward the backstage, Camden grabbed at Lukas's arm to urge him to follow. But Lukas, lit torch in hand and a mouth full of paraffin, wouldn't budge. He was too petrified to move and held out the torch like someone trying to ward off a vampire. When the mob finished with the twins and rounded on him, Lukas finally remembered to scream. He opened his mouth, but instead of sound, the paraffin emerged, combusting against the torch. A ball of flame scorched the stage. Unfortunately for Lukas, this flame barely slowed the mob down. All it managed to do was catch the tent wall on fire. The tarpaulin went up like dry cotton, belching black plastic smoke.

Seeing that the situation was futile, Camden made his exit. There was only one space left on the proverbial life raft and he intended to plant his butt firmly in that seat. Before he disappeared backstage, he looked over his shoulder a final time. Through the veil of smoke and flames, he saw the mob drag Lukas down. They stomped him like a sack of grapes for wine of gruesome vintage.

*　　*　　*

Camden burst through the back of the tent. His eyes burned. His lungs felt like he'd freebased an exhaust pipe. He had lost his big green wig in the smoke and confusion. Wheezing and hacking, he staggered into the middle of the road. A ribbon of saliva hung from his lips, forming a ladder of drool that reached the ground. He made pitiful raspberries to dislodge the spittle. Wiping his mouth with the back of his hand, he looked back at the burning tent, and wondered how a little clowning could go so wrong.

He was unsure of where to go or what to do. The twins, Lukas – they were all gone. And to make matters, if not worse, then more uncomfortable, he had, judging by the slick between his thighs, finally cleared the blockage in his bowels. Who knows how long he might have stood in the road, drooling and shit-caked, had someone not called to him.

"Psst! Cammy. Over here!"

Camden squinted into the darkness towards the direction of the voice. In the moonlight, he saw two heads peeking out from behind a bald palm tree. With a wide gait to prevent his sticky thighs from touching, he bowlegged his way to the

116

tree. He found Piper hiding there, safe and sound. For better or worse, he also found Jody, who for some reason was still carrying his devil stick.

"Thank god, you're alright, Cammy," Piper said. "Where are the others? Lukas? The twins?"

"They didn't make it," Camden said, struggling to find the rights words. "They're. . . they're still inside."

"They're in the tent?" Piper asked, staring at the smoke billowing from the big top. "You just left them? They need our help. Something terrible could happen to them!"

"We're kind of past that point now," Camden said. "Something terrible already did."

"You mean . . ." Piper began but stopped. The question was too terrible to ask, and she didn't want to hear the answer.

Not knowing what to say, Camden looked down at his bright red clown shoes and nodded.

Piper exhibited the classic symptoms of shock. Her lower lip trembled. Her face went pale. Her features assumed a pitiful expression as though she had sat in a bowl of cold jello.

"How could this happen?" she whispered. "Lukas. The twins. All of this violence. I just don't believe it." She shook her head, breaking off.

Camden looked at Piper with infinite sympathy. She seemed so helpless and lost. Forgetting himself for the moment – the death, the destruction, the shit between his thighs – he reached out and touched her softly on the arm. He was fully prepared to transition that consoling touch to a hug or even more. You know, wherever Piper wanted to take things.

Unfortunately, Piper did not want to take things anywhere. At least not with Camden. She sought comfort from another source. She turned from Camden and fell into Jody's arms.

"We came all this way," Piper said, pressing her head against Jody's chest. "We worked so hard. We only wanted to bring joy. To shine a little light in a dark world. And this is what happened? This is how they repaid us? I can't believe it."

As she spoke, her eyes fluttered in her sockets like light-drunk moths. That anyone, let alone a people as hopeless and deprived as the Mbanzans, might reject her plucky desire to make good, would not lodge in her brain. That notion was completely incompatible with Piper's conception of herself and her special place in the world.

"Neither can I," Jody said as he ran his fingers through her hair. "You try to make the world a better place. To help someone. But some people just don't want to be helped."

"How can people be so ungrateful?" she asked. "Is it wrong that I'm hurt? Is it wrong that I feel this way?"

Jody took Piper by her slender shoulders and gave her a rousing little shake. He gazed deep into her eyes. "There are no wrong feelings, babe," he said. "Feelings are never wrong."

If feelings were never wrong, Camden was a corpse. Because, as he looked on Piper and Jody, he felt dead inside. Their display of affection was almost as scarring to watch as the mob that tore apart Lukas and the twins. The only saving grace about both terrible scenes was that they were mercifully brief. Piper and Jody's passion play was cut short by developments across the road. The tent flap entrance was thrown open and the mob, worked into a rabid lather, started to spill out. With their silhouettes cast by the flames and shrouded in smoke, they looked like a legion of imps from a Hieronymus Bosch fever dream. But whereas those quaint Flemish demons were outfitted with period spears and pitchforks, this mob had modern firepower. Having looted the bodies of the fallen peacekeepers, they were armed with shiny new machine guns and lightly-used blue helmets.

The surviving members of *Cirque du Poverte, Part Deux* shrank behind the tree and considered their options.

118

"What are we going to do?" Piper asked.

"We can't stay here," Camden said. "I saw what those people could do before they had guns. We need to get out of here."

"But where can we go?" Piper asked. "Jody, where should we go?"

"I don't know," Jody muttered. "I'm thinking. I need time to think." He chewed his lower lips and rubbed the shaggy head of his devil stick in intense contemplation. After a moment, his brow furled with resolve. He'd reached a decision.

"We need to run," he said.

"That's not much of a plan," Camden said, underwhelmed by the proposal. "But the question is where to?"

"Who cares? Anywhere has to be better than this," Jody said. Without further prologue, he grabbed Piper's arm and pulled her to her feet. They fled down the shadowy side of the road, away from the burning tent and the mob.

Camden had no choice but to follow. He got into his clown shoes and waddled after them.

Piper and Jody ran ahead, hand-in-hand, as Camden trailed behind. In the receding distance, the tent was in full flame. The canvas flared and billowed like the sail of a doomed ship.

As they raced towards the unknown, Piper turned to Jody, "Where does this road go?" she asked.

"I don't know," Jody said. "But every road leads somewhere, right?"

"Doo-doo-doo-da-doo-doo-daaaah!" Olson sang at his desk in the Fistula Initiative.

"Doo-doo-doo-da-doo-doo-daaaah!" the tinny computer speakers echoed back, accompanied by one of the cornier polyrhythms to ever disgrace 80's radio.

"Doo-doo-doo-da-doo-doo-daaaah!" Olson repeated without shame.

"Doo-doo-doo-da-doo-doo-daaaah!" the computer replied a final time. The track's percussive intro faded into a twinkling run of digital xylophones. The first verse of Toto's *Africa* rang out, "I hear the drums echo in the night . . ."

The song continued on in this vein, appropriating African clichés and mixing them liberally with casual racisms. Olson, however, had stopped singing along to the internet radio. Having already sung for some time, his throat has dry. He took a break from his one-man karaoke and refreshed himself with his rum cocktail. He reclined in his chair, smacked his lips, and savored the moment.

Two drinks deep towards alcoholic bliss, Olson regarded his nearly empty glass and looked forward to his third. He was in a good mood, which was not like him at all. It had been a long time since he felt giddy enough to sing with the radio and had the office to himself to actually do it. Although he was appreciably buzzed, his fuzzy feelings only partially resulted from the Tipo Tipico that sloshed around his stomach. His wellspring of happiness was the fact that the mission was finally over.

Olson looked over at the clock on the wall. Kruger must have delivered the shipment by now. In all likelihood, Congolo had distributed the weapons. Poorly-trained soldiers were probably already shooting themselves in the feet with their new machine guns. Thankfully, the competence of the Mbanzan military was not Olson's responsibility. He just ran the guns – he did not make sure that their recipients could use them.

Olson leaned back and luxuriated in the satisfaction of a job well done. No, his life circumstances had not changed. He was still in his African exile, and Mbanza was the same armpit it had been. But as Sisyphus learned as he strolled down the hill after that boulder with a whistle on his lips, even hell has its moments. Reaching for the bottle of Tipo Tipico, Olson could relate. For the first time in months, Gary was not in the command center, fiddling with his drones or playing his Xbox. Olson was alone, free to drink, crank up the radio, and sing Toto as he pleased.

He mouthed along to the chorus, blessing rains down in Africa, as he prepared a third beverage. He raised the drink to his lips and nodded approvingly. Just the way he liked it. Heavy on the Tipo Tipico with just a splash of mango juice to take the edge off the gut-rot. But as the alcohol traveled through his veins, spreading warmly from his chest to his toes, unwanted thoughts invaded the happy haze. Even as he nodded his head to the music, Olson glanced involuntarily at the dark command center across the hall. Despite increasingly frequent sips of his drink, he could not silence the nagging voice in his ear, whispering: "Where the hell was Gary?"

Olson looked at his watch. It was getting late. His office had no windows, but it must be dark. The show should have ended long ago. Gary should already be hanging around outside Olson's door, blabbering about the evils of alcohol or his weird clown fixation. Instead, he was out in Mbanza somewhere. And Mbanza was not a safe place at night for a person like Gary. In terms of the world's most dangerous places, Olson would put Mbanza somewhere with Tegucigalpa (Honduras), Kabul (Afghanistan), and Toledo (Ohio), a Gorgon's gala of sister cities if there had ever been one. Olson took another drink, but the fuzzy feelings were gone. Despite his best efforts to get obliviously drunk, Africa had managed to creep into his thoughts, ruining an otherwise lovely evening.

Olson grudgingly set his drink aside and wondered what could have happened to Gary. Just as something resembling concern set in, he noticed his cell phone ringing on his desk. Thanks to the high volume of Toto, he hadn't noticed it before. The phone buzzed and jittered like an epileptic on St. Vitus Day. Thinking that it could be Gary, he snatched up the phone. He was annoyed to see Congolo's number on the display.

Olson answered, prepared to hang up as soon as possible. "Now is not a good time, Congolo," he said. "I have other things to do than listen to you gloat about the guns or the glories of Mbanza."

Congolo did not respond with his usual bloviation. But Olson got another kind of earful. Bedlam boomed through the cell phone, as though Olson had been connected to a universe of chaos and static. He heard shouting, crashing, and the sound of gunfire. Congolo's voice barely registered against the ambient violence.

"Olson, is that you?" Congolo asked breathlessly. "Thank god you picked up. I have been calling you for . . ."

A loud explosion forced Olson to remove the phone from his ear. When he returned it to listen, Congolo was raving. "We need your help!" he cried. "They're overrunning the station!"

"Slow down," Olson commanded. "What's going on? Who is overrunning what?"

"The police station is under attack. . . The riot . . . The whole town . . . rebellion!" Congolo explained, his voice cutting in and out.

"What are you talking about?" Olson grumbled, struggling to wrap his wet brain around the situation. "I'm in Mbanza. I'm sitting right here. I don't notice any rebellion."

"We are trapped in the police station," Congolo repeated as if he hadn't heard Olson. "We are surrounded. You must help us!" he begged. A hail of machinegun fire punctuated the request.

"Congolo, listen to me," Olson said, trying to sound as reassuring and sober as possible. "If there is a situation, you're calling the wrong guy. I'm one man. Putting down uprisings is not my line of work. You need to get on the phone with your army. You need to call the capital."

Congolo cursed into the phone. "There is no time. We need help this minute!" His voice was filled with fear and frustration. "Send the drones. Send the tank. Do you see now? This is why I needed a tank!"

"I've told you before," Olson said. "You're not getting a tank!"

"For the love of God, send the tank!" Congolo shouted before his voice cut out a final time.

The line was dead. With a trembling hand, Olson set the cell phone down. He swallowed a little rum that had returned to his throat during the conversation. He slumped in his chair, his face as white as a ghost. "It's not possible," he muttered. "It's Benghazi all over again."

14

A head shorter than the crowd around him, Jammu did not have a clear sightline to the stage. But he did not need an unobstructed view to know that something terrible had happened. The Mbanzans jostled and frothed like an angry sea as they pressed towards the front of the tent. There were shouts. There were screams. And then there was fire. The stage burst into flames that quickly climbed the tarpaulin walls, casting the tent in a hellish Halloween orange.

Years of hunger, privation, and desperation boiled over as a rage swept through the crowd that was as contagious as typhoid and as fatal as Ebola. To Jammu, it seemed as though every Mbanzan had lost their mind. As tried to keep hold of the rope around his goat's neck, he thought he was the only one immune to the madness.

Jammu was wrong. At least one other person in the tent had not been infected by the bloodlust. Lurking in the dark corner, still wearing a straw hat and holding a bag of peanuts, Gary was profoundly out of place in a riot. He was dressed for a Sunday picnic, not civil unrest. As the situation on the stage turned lethal, Gary had tried not to move a muscle, operating under the desperate notion that, if he

123

stood still enough, no one would notice him. Evidenced by the fact that he was still alive, the strategy had paid off so far. But as the fire raced across the ceiling of the tent, Gary decided it was time to go. He noticed Jammu leading his goat along the wall, sneaking towards the back of the tent. Gary concluded that the African boy had the right idea and followed.

When Jammu sensed someone behind him, he nearly jumped out of his skin. But when he turned, he at once recognized Gary as the man who had kindly shared his peanuts before the show. The fear passed and the two exchanged a look that communicated their shock and bewilderment. Each experienced a sense of relief at the realization they were not the only sane person left in Mbanza. But this moment of consolation was fleeting. For just as Jammu and Gary found each other, the mob took notice.

Having made short work of the peacekeepers and all the performers they could get their hands on, the Mbanzans were casting about the tent, looking for something else to smash. That was when they came across Jammu and Gary. Gary's pudgy face and wide waist screamed soft target. Jammu was damned by association. And the goat was, well, a goat. A detachment separated from the main group and blocked the exit. The rest of the mob encircled their would-be victims and collapsed with a slow, inevitable menace.

Jammu was petrified and unable to move as the mob bore down. But, fortunately for Jammu, Gary was not as soft a target as his physique suggested. As the mob raised their fists and prepared to pounce, Gary reacted with unexpected speed, exhibiting reflexes that had been sharpened by countless hours of Xbox. With the swiftness of a ninja, he lifted his bag of peanuts and threw it into the face of an oncoming attacker. The paper bag exploded as it struck the Mbanzan, showering peanuts across the tent floor.

It may have only been peanuts, but it was enough to divert a famished mob that had not eaten in days. The Mbanzans stared down at the food, torn between their hunger for vengeance and the gnawing emptiness in their stomachs. It wasn't much of an opening, but it was enough. Evincing the dash of a man half his size, Gary pushed through his assailants, not towards the exit, but into the cloud of smoke rapidly filling the tent, disappearing into the acrid blackness.

Jammu, also half-starved, gawked at the scattered peanuts along with the rest of the Mbanzans. But while he was distracted, his little goat, alarmed by the fire and sensing the mob's intention that it should be dinner, bolted for the exit. Jammu, still holding the goat's rope in his hand, was dragged in tow.

It took all of Jammu's speed and concentration to keep up with the goat as it weaved through the mob. Having personally dragged the stubborn beast halfway across the savanna, he had no idea that four shaggy hooves could normally generate such velocity. But these, of course, were not normal conditions. In a reversal of roles, the goatherd was led by his flock – or at least its last surviving member. The little goat lowered its nubby horns and beelined for the open tent flap, ramming through every shin in its way. The goat was less an animal than some sort of cloven bulldozer, plowing through the mob and through the exit, emerging into the night.

The goat dragged Jammu down the road and showed no signs of stopping. As they fled, carnage followed on their heels. The mob – many armed with clubs and machine guns – flooded the street. The surrounding slums were already catching fire – whether caused by sparks from the burning tent or intentionally spread was unclear. But even motivated by a well-developed sense of survival, a determined goat could only go so far. Goats, regardless of their other advantages, were not built for distance running. Before long, the animal's legs started to wobble. And then the animal collapsed. Jammu picked up his shaggy friend and tried to carry on, despite the pain in his clubfoot. But even he had reached his limit. Jammu's lungs burned. His chest throbbed. His pace slowed. The sounds of destruction started to overtake them, but Jammu could go no farther. He stumbled and slumped down in the center of the road.

With his goat by his side, Jammu lay on his back in the red dirt, gasping for breath. The slums burned around him. The sounds of gunfire echoed from every direction. Panting and wheezing, Jammu became convinced that his death was imminent. He gazed up into the sky and resolved to spend his final moments in quiet contemplation of Nana. Despite his youth, he was not afraid of dying. Frankly, his life had been a luckless affair, even by sub-Saharan standards. He only regretted that he had not been strong enough to save Nana from Teacher Mapouro. As he regarded the stars, Jammu prayed that he and Nana might be reunited in the afterlife. But an unwelcome thought presented itself. If she were to marry Teacher Mapouro in this world, would she be his bride in the next? Must she be Mapouro's wife for eternity? Would Jammu be denied his love and happiness for all time?

As Jammu agonized over the marital conventions of the hereafter, the chaos closed in from all sides. He could feel the heat from the fires. He heard distinct voices moving up the street. The ground shook, sending tremors through his chest. He assumed that death had arrived and that the Earth was about to swallow him whole.

But Jammu was mistaken. Death had not arrived. What he felt was 25 tons of mechanized armor rolling through Mbanza. Jammu lifted his head from the road and looked towards the intersection. A long metal barrel emerged from behind a shack. The barrel swiveled tentatively from side to side, as though it could not decide which direction to turn. After some indecision, the rest of the tank rumbled into the intersection and pivoted towards Jammu. The goatherd watched its approach with detachment. The tank was a monster of a machine and its size was exaggerated by wooden crates strapped to its sides, stacked high like Jenga blocks.

Despite lying in the tank's path, Jammu did not try to get out of the way. His body trembled. His teeth chattered in his skull. But aside from these involuntary vibrations, he did not flinch. Resigned to an early death, Jammu regarded the tank with a mix of curiosity and fatalism. In particular, he focused on the metal plates of the tank tread rolling his way. Jammu welcomed them, reasoning that those tracks would offer a quick and more merciful death than the mob ravaging the town. Given the current circumstances, being crushed by a tank was probably the best option he could reasonably hope for. He took a deep breath, closed his eyes, and tried to think of Nana.

Having made his peace, Jammu was almost disappointed when the tank shuddered to a stop, only feet from his limp body. There was a creak of metal and then a bang. There was a click in the darkness and then Jammu was bathed in spotlight's halo. Jammu shaded his eyes with his hands and peered past the beam. An enormous silhouette emerged from a hatch on the tank. The spotlight swiveled and caught a red-faced man with an eyepatch, regarding Jammu with good-natured disbelief.

"You again?" Kruger called down to Jammu. "Do you make a habit of winding up in the worst situations? Never mind, I don't care. Just tell me, how the hell do you get out of this damn town!"

15

The SUV crawled across the plaza towards the police station. Even with his vision bleary with half a bottle of Tipo Tipico, Olson could see that all was not well. The floodlights on the roof had been cut and the square was dark. The checkpoints and the sandbag perimeter were unmanned. His headlights reflected off bullet casings that twinkled among the cobblestones. As he inched the SUV forward, he saw that the station's front door was caved in as if someone had taken a batting ram to it. He gripped the steering wheel tightly, seeking confidence in the vehicle's 8-cylinder engine and bulletproofing.

Olson intended to make this a quick stop. Parking in the shadows, he slipped from the SUV and crept through the splintered front door into the station. He met no resistance in the lobby. The front desk was empty. Even the stray dogs that usually spent the night on the benches had seen fit to scram.

Relying on his training and, more importantly, a courage fueled by several stiff drinks, Olson traveled from the lobby into the back offices. The lights were on, but again no one was home. By the looks of things, the place had been deserted in a hurry. Olson had missed the action, but not by much. The air stunk of sulphur and gunpowder. Fresh bullet holes gouged the faded walls, and plaster dust still pollinated the air. Windows were broken. Chairs were smashed. As Olson progressed, he walked through loose files and carbon forms in triplicate that covered the floor like shavings in a hamster cage.

Olson stood ankle deep in debris, considering his options. The fate of the police force was not entirely clear, but, judging by their headquarters, they didn't seem likely to quell any rebellions. Increasingly, Mbanza looked like a lost cause. And the prospects of finding Congolo were equally dim. If Congolo had any brains, he'd be in a car racing away across the savannah. If he didn't, he was probably already dead. In either case, Olson wasn't going to chase after him.

Having reached this conclusion, Olson decided it was time to make his own exit. Jogging back through the station, he considered his odds and figured they weren't half bad. Granted, his confidence was inflated by rum, and things evidently had gone poorly for a better armed, and more numerous police force, but Olson had certain advantages that the Mbanzan authorities lacked. The most important of these was an armor-plated SUV with a full tank of gas. Even with its miserable fuel-efficiency, Olson could make it out of Mbanza and to the capitol, or even to the border, which might be necessary depending on how far the unrest had spread.

The SUV was his ace in the hole. Olson wouldn't have given it up for the world. Yet, pleased as he was to have an escape plan, he couldn't shake a touch of survivor's remorse. It was hard to get too worked up about Congolo – the man deserved no sympathy – but Gary was another matter. Olson hated to think of him out there alone while Mbanza went to hell. Gary may have dropped bombs on people for a living, but he was nice enough otherwise. And it wasn't like Gary picked the targets. He was just a man doing his unconsidered duty, which wasn't that different than any other schlub. And then there were the clowns, who Olson remembered with a cringe. Those kids were idiots and had no business in Mbanza. They didn't deserve what was coming to them though. Still, in this part of the world, deserve had nothing to do with it.

Olson tried to ignore these complications as he raced through the abandoned station. He had no doubt that he would feel awful about Gary and the others tomorrow. But there were worse things than guilt. Unlike a half-baked rescue mission into a burning town, a little more guilt would not kill him. It was also a consolation that there was not much he could do, even if he wanted to. If Gary and the clowns were still alive – which was a big, honking *if* – Olson didn't know where they were. Ultimately, this plausible uncertainty would have allowed him to jump into his SUV and escape across the savanna in armor-plated, air-conditioned comfort. But before Olson could slip out of Mbanza with only a slightly-soiled conscience, the ethical equation got more complicated. As he approached the lobby, Olson heard muffled screams behind him in the station. He paused. He cursed as he realized the screams came from the holding cells.

The steel door groaned as it opened, unmuffling the cries for help. Olson was subjected to full-throated shouts as he stepped into the jail. When the police fled, they left the prisoners behind. And those prisoners, aware that things had gone to hell, were beating against the bars and begging to be released.

Olson appreciated their position. Being locked in a jail during a revolt must have felt like being lashed to a sinking ship. But although he sympathized with the prisoners' plight, he'd be a fool to release them. Justice in Mbanza was anything but discriminating, but there were surely a few bad apples in those overcrowded cells. Statistically speaking, a corrupt police force has to catch an actual criminal from time to time. By keeping the cells locked and preserving a firm, metal iron between himself and the prisoner population, Olson could control at least one variable in an otherwise fubar situation. Besides, the prisoners were probably safer in the jail than out on the street. It's not as if they'd starve to death in their cells. Olson was reasonably certain that someone else would come along eventually. That would most likely be the case. At the very least, the possibility existed.

Sufficiently convinced that he wasn't consigning a cellblock to death, Olson turned to go. But his overdue escape was further delayed when one of the prisoners addressed him directly in French with a god-awful accent.

"Ibrahim, Ibrahim! You must help me, Ibrahim! Don't forget your poor brother, Unrice!"

It took Olson a moment to recognize the African pressed against the cell door. During the excitement of the last few days, he had completely forgotten about the master criminals, Unrice and Maurice. In his defense, Unrice had seen better days. The police habitually threw the book at suspects, but it looked like they'd dropped a whole library on Unrice. His bruised face looked like an eggplant. His right eye was swollen shut, and his eyebrow had been replaced by a bright red gash. His dirty farm fingers – intermittently dislocated and denailed – resembled worms coiled around the prison bars.

Despite his shattered appearance, however, Unrice's will had not been broken. He was in remarkably high spirits, all things considered.

"Thank god you are here, Ibrahim. I knew that you would return. See Maurice, I said he would return!" Ibrahim spoke to the African beside him. Maurice no longer towered over his shorter friend. By the looks of things, he had gotten it even worse than Unrice. He hung limply from the cell bars. Whether he could stand was unclear.

"See Maurice, I told you he was a good man!" Unrice cried in his own dialect.

Maurice did not voice an opinion on the subject. He regarded Olson with glassy eyes. He looked like a fish lying on the shore, slowly suffocating.

130

Olson frowned as he considered their sorry states. "You two look like hell. You didn't follow my advice, did you? You should have confessed. I told you to tell them whatever they wanted to hear."

"But Ibrahim, they wanted me to say that I was a terrorist," Unrice protested. "How can I tell them that? How could I lie about such a thing?"

"You lied to me about a lot of things when we first met," Olson said.

"That was different," Unrice said. "You offered me so much money to say those things. But the police, they offered me nothing. Not a penny! I would not condemn myself for nothing. I have my principles."

"A whole lot of good your principles did you," Olson said.

"Perhaps. But none of that matters now. You are here. God sent you to deliver us. You are our savior. I never doubted you. Maurice, didn't I say that I never doubted him?" he asked, nudging his unresponsive friend.

"Alright, okay. I get it. Enough with that already," Olson said. "What happened here? Where are the police?"

"I don't know," Unrice said. "There were terrible noises outside the door: shouting, gunfire, explosions. The guards fled. And then everything went quiet."

"They didn't say where they were going?" Olson asked.

"Why would they tell us? They just left."

Olson nodded. "Alright, listen to me, Unrice. I'm sure the capital is sending reinforcements as we speak. This situation will blow over soon enough. Just stay where you are and hold tight. Everything will be okay."

"You aren't going to let me out?" Unrice asked. "You're leaving me here?"

"That's right," Olson said. "Wait for the army to come. You'll be fine."

"How will I be fine?" Unrice asked with confusion. "The government thinks I'm a terrorist. Staying here is a death sentence. I want to go home to my village. To my children. To my wives."

Olson wanted to help Unrice. He really did. He couldn't help feeling partly to blame for the man's predicament. But if he opened the cell door, Unrice would not

131

be the only one coming out. It was almost certain that some of the other prisoners had caught the riot spirit coursing through Mbanza. Retribution was in the air. Even now, some of the Africans eyed Olson in a deeply unsettling way. If the prisoners had an appetite for destruction, he didn't want to be the first person they met when they left their cells.

"Trust me, Unrice. You don't want to leave this station. It's safer in that cell," Olson said, without specifying for whom it was safer.

"I'm safer here? Look at my face. Look at my fingers," Unrice said, thrusting his broken hand past the bars. "Things could not be worse than here."

"I wouldn't be so sure," Olson said. "The town is a war zone. Everything has gone to hell. It's a powder keg that's started to blow out there." Then, as if underscoring his point, an explosion rocked the building. Even in the jail, sheltered in the interior of the station, the walls shook and chunks of plaster fell from the ceiling. The air filled with thick white dust.

As Olson recovered from the blast, something tickled his nose. It was the smell of burning gasoline. A bad feeling bubbled up in his stomach. "Hold that thought," he muttered as he ran out of the cell block.

"My brother, Ibrahim," Unrice cried after him. "Where are you going? You can't leave us!"

But Olson had already gone. He retraced his steps to the lobby. The scene he found was not encouraging. It looked like a tornado had torn through the room. The front desk was wrecked. The benches were broken against the far wall. The splintered door to the plaza was replaced by a frame of fire. Olson approached the door reluctantly. The air reeked of petroleum. He covered his mouth and nose and squinted through the burning exit. His worst fear was confirmed.

The shadow where he had parked his SUV was no longer a shadow. And the SUV was no longer an SUV. It was an armor-plated bonfire, burning brightly in the cobblestone square. The vehicle may have been bullet proof, but it was clearly not flame retardant. In the flickering light, Olson made out figures marching across the plaza. They carried torches and clubs. Some were dressed in scraps of police uniforms, an odd helmet here and a shirt with epaulettes there. A few even had machine guns that they fired into the sky in deranged celebration.

As the mob neared the station, a scrap of dirty white caught Olson's eye. He thought it was some banner at first. But he quickly realized that it was no banner. It was a soiled white suit. In that moment, the mystery of Congolo's whereabouts was solved. The mob had him, or what was left of him anyway, and was hoisting him like a balloon in a ghoulish parade. From his vantage through the burning door, Olson wasn't sure if Congolo was alive or dead, but he hoped for Congolo's sake it was the latter. As he peered through the smoke and fire, he saw Congolo's mouth open. Olson thought he might scream until a hand reached out, grabbed Congolo by the teeth, and dragged him below the crowd.

Olson retreated from the door and tried to forget about Congolo. With the SUV a flaming wreck, the possibility of simply driving out of Mbanza was gone. Olson needed a new plan, but there were no good options. As he considered the hopeless situation, the lobby got hotter and filled with smoke. Olson realized that the police station was on fire. Flames had spread from the burning door across the walls. Olson swore. It wasn't enough that he had to figure out how to escape Mbanza. Now he had to worry about the prisoners locked in their cells. He sighed as he watched the flames lick the ceiling. With a heavy heart, he realized what he had to do.

When Olson returned to the jail, the prisoners were in a state. They knew that the station was on fire. The jail was smoky and hotter by several degrees. The air had the subtle whiff of burning Barbie dolls.

"Ibrahim, you have returned!" Unrice cried when he saw Olson. "I knew you would not leave us!"

Olson did not respond. Resigned to the danger he was exposing himself to, he went about the grim duty of saving lives. He found a set of keys hanging from the wall. A heavy iron bar was locked across the cell door, holding it in place. Olson cursed himself as he undid the lock. He took a deep breath and opened the door. He hoped that he would not have to pay too high a price for this uncharacteristic display of compassion.

Unfortunately, Olson had always been an excellent judge of character. Once the cell door was open, half a dozen prisoners swarmed him. He barely had time to throw up his hands before he was knocked to the floor. Assuming the fetal position – a preferred defensive stance for both bear attacks and angry mobs – he weathered a storm of pounding fists and stomping feet. But, as luck would have it, the violence turned out to be more of a cloudburst. The prisoners had been, after all, starved and beaten. They were physically capable of inflicting only so much damage, and they did not have a lot of time to do it. No one had forgotten that the station was on fire. Ultimately, the imperative to flee a burning building won out over the desire to beat a stranger.

The assault may have been brief, but Olson still saw stars after the prisoners fled. He emerged from his protective crouch, bloodied and dizzy. On some level, his contused brain knew that he needed to leave the station. But he had no idea how to manage an escape when the room would not stop spinning. Consequently, he was surprised when someone grabbed his arms, lifted him to his feet, and dragged him out of the jail. Olson stared vaguely at two pairs of filthy farmers' hands supporting his shoulders. He looked at the hands' owners. To his left, he recognized Maurice, who apparently could walk. To his right, he saw Unrice, who smiled back toothlessly. Olson experienced a complicated emotion, a mixture of gratitude, relief, shame, and a sincere hope that Unrice had lost those teeth coming to Mbanza.

As soon as Olson was dragged outside, the station burst into flames. He could feel the heat on his back as the Africans guided him across the cobblestones like a loose-limbed drunk. When they reached the center of the square, Unrice and Maurice laid him in the shadow of the Morgan Freeman Memorial Zulu statue.

Still experiencing a disconnect between his brain and body after his beating, Olson looked stupidly at the men who had saved his life. Maurice pulled at Unrice's arm, urging him to leave. "We must go, my brother," Unrice said, with genuine regret in his voice. "We can carry you no farther. And we must leave before the government returns. Stay out of sight. Stay in the shadows. May God protect you!"

Unrice continued to mutter to this effect as Maurice pulled him away. Eventually, both men broke into a run. Olson watched them as they disappeared into the darkness.

Olson did as he was told. He stayed out of sight. Concealed in the statue's shadow, he watched the police station burn. In his concussed state, he was unfazed by the gunshots and explosions that echoed through the old town. He wasn't even bothered by the menacing shadows that lurked along the edges of the square. Olson knew that he couldn't stay where he was, but he had nowhere else to go. For lack of a better option, he defaulted towards inaction.

But this changed when Olson noticed a rumbling. The cobblestones vibrated beneath his hands and legs. A faint mechanical drone steadily built into a roar. Olson hardly believed his eyes when he saw a tank burst into the plaza. He watched in disbelief as the tank proceeded to lap the square like a car stuck circling a roundabout.

It gradually dawned on Olson that he knew this tank. There was, of course, only one tank anywhere near Mbanza. Moreover, there was only one other person, aside from himself, who knew where the tank was hidden. Olson slowly realized that this tank was his ticket out of town, his best and last chance. While the tank's appearance seemed a little too convenient, and Olson could not discount the possibility that it was all a hallucination in his tenderized brain, that was a chance he had to take.

Olson struggled to his feet and started after the tank, which was taking another pass around the plaza. He moved unsteadily on his legs. Stumbling forward and waving his arms, he screamed after the tank, "Stop the tank, Kruger! Don't leave me here! Turn that tank around!"

Unfortunately, the tank did not turn around. To Olson's profound disappointment, it rumbled across the square a final time before turning and disappearing down a side street. Kruger had not seen him, but Olson did catch someone else's attention. As Olson stood in the open, trying in vain to hail the tank, a muzzle flare flashed in the darkness. Olson faintly registered the sound of a gunshot before what felt like a baseball bat struck his jaw and the cobblestones rushed up towards him.

16

Contrary to Jody's assertion, not every road goes somewhere. Sometimes they just stop. The Wanda Road was one such road. What began promisingly as a broad stretch of red dirt leading out of Mbanza ended in disappointment. The road extended less than a mile before it was swallowed by the savanna and terminated abruptly at a dwarf acacia tree.

Camden limped towards Jody and Piper, who had already reached the tree. If there had been any doubt before, Camden now knew through excruciating first-hand knowledge that clown shoes were not designed for overland travel. He moved with the graceless waddle of an arthritic duck. And if his running form looked bad, it felt even worse. The plastic shoes sawed into his ankles, filleting the backs of his heels. But Camden did not slow down. His heels were a small price to pay to save the rest of his skin. If circumstances demanded it, he would have run until the plastic ate clean through his ankles and his feet came off.

As Camden approached Piper and Jody, he tried to hide the tears in his eyes. But his attempt to put on a brave face was undermined when he collapsed on the road, unable to take another step in the damned shoes. For better or worse, he needn't have bothered to look tough. Piper and Jody paid him no mind. Wrapped in an embrace, they stared back down the road, watching Mbanza burn. Despite the horror and destruction, their faces seemed relaxed as though they were watching fireworks or a bonfire on the beach.

"The fire is everywhere," Piper said with a curious detachment. "Everything is burning."

"It's spreading up the hill," Jody said, indicating the path of destruction with his devil stick. "It's moving fast. By tomorrow, there won't be anything left."

Piper pulled herself closer, barnacling to Jody. "It's so bright. Like a sunset."

"Or a sunrise," Jody replied.

"It's almost beautiful," she said.

"Yes, it is."

"But terrible too," she added.

"It's so terrible," Jody agreed, squeezing her solemnly.

"We could still be back there in that burning tent," Piper said. "That could have been us. We could have ended up like the others. . . like . . . ." She shook her head. "It's just too terrible."

"Thank god we made it," Jody said.

"No, thank you, Jody," Piper said. "If it wasn't for you, we'd still be back there. You got us away to safety."

Camden was still sitting in the road. His shoes were off. To distract himself from Jody and Piper's conversation, he fingered the flayed skin on his heels. He now tore himself away from his masochistic inspection to bear bad news.

"I hate to break it to you, but don't get too comfortable. We're not out of the woods yet."

"What are you talking about?" Piper asked. "We're safe where we are. Mbanza is way over there. And we're all the way over here."

"What happens when they're finished with the town?" Camden asked. "Where are they going to go next?"

Jody made a skeptical raspberry. "Africa is a big place," he said, waiving his devil stick in a 360 arc. "Look around. The savanna goes in every direction. What are the odds they'll find us here?"

"Pretty good, I'd think," Camden said. "There aren't too many roads leading out of town. If they follow this one, it leads right to us."

"Don't be so hysterical," Jody said. "We're fine."

Jody was unmoved. But peevish doubt flashed across Piper's face. She had convinced herself that she was safe and secure in Jody's arms. The suggestion that she was still in danger was not appreciated.

"Why are you saying these things, Cammy?" Piper snapped. "Is this about Jody? Is this about me? Is this about us being together? Because if it is, it's really starting to get old."

Whether it was his recent brush with death or his mangled feet, Camden had no capacity to dance around Piper's feelings anymore. He spoke plainly. "Piper, I can promise you that, for the first time on this trip, what I'm saying has nothing to do with you or Jody. This has everything to do with me. And not wanting to die. You might feel safe right now. But in a few hours, that sun is going to come up. And when it does, we're going to be sitting ducks unless we think of something."

Piper frowned. Camden had given her something bitter to chew on. For her twenty-something years living on this Earth, she had forgotten that the sun eventually rises. Even now, beyond the blazing town in the middle distance, there was a faint, but unmistakable, brightening on the horizon.

Jody was still not convinced. "Sunrise? I'm sure this will all work out by then. We just need to keep our heads down and sit tight. The army is probably on its way right now. I'm sure that this whole situation will get sorted out in no time."

"How are you so positive?" Camden said. "On what basis do you believe that there is anyone coming here to help us?"

"It's just what armies do," Jody said.

Despite Jody's confidence, Piper was increasingly skeptical. She wriggled from his warm embrace and confronted the cold-hard facts. "Jody, maybe Cammy is onto something. Maybe we should have some sort of plan other than sitting here and waiting."

"Not you too, Piper," Jody said with a chuckle. "Don't let him freak you out. We're fine. Don't you trust me, babe?"

"Sure, I trust you," she said. "You got us this far. And you're probably right. I'm sure the army is coming right now. But is a backup plan really a bad idea?"

Jody chuckled. "Okay, let's have a backup plan then," he said, as though humoring a child.

Facing north, he began to assess their options. "What should we do? Where should we go, hmm? I see some mountains. Not much else," he said.

There is a whole lot of nothing over there," he said, turning clockwise and waving his devil stick in an easterly direction.

He looked to the south. "That's Mbanza. That's on fire. We can't go there."

"More of absolutely nothing," he said, surveying the west.

"And, yup, there are those mountains again," he said, completing his rotation. "It seems to me there is nowhere to go. I guess we're staying here."

"Even if there is nowhere to go, we could at least get out of the road," Piper said. "Maybe walk a little into the savanna?"

"Have you seen how thick this grass is?" Jody whacked the brush that lined the road with his devil stick. "How far do you think we'd get?"

"As the person with bleeding feet," Camden said, "I'm the last one that wants to stomp through that grass. But I'm willing to make that sacrifice considering the circumstances."

Jody shook his head. His manbun bounced pessimistically. "Are you sure? Who knows what's out there? Snakes. Scorpions. There might even be a lion."

"Who cares what *might* be out there?" Camden said. "We know for a fact what's in that town, and what they'll do if they find us. I'll take my chances with the lion."

"You're talking crazy. Now is not the time to panic," Jody said.

"I disagree," Camden said. "This is the perfect time to panic. There has never been a better time to panic."

"Just stop it," Piper commanded. "Both of you. You're talking in circles. There must be something we can do."

"We can hide," Camden volunteered. He pointed to the dwarf acacia. "Look at that tree. Maybe we could all hide behind it."

"And how long would we have to hide?" Piper asked.

"For as long as it takes," Camden said.

"It would never work," Jody said, splashing cold water on the idea. "It's too small. It's not big enough for one of us, let alone three."

"Maybe we should backtrack?" Piper suggested. "Maybe we missed a turn or something? Maybe there is another road?"

"There was no other road," Camden said.

"It's dark. We might have missed it," she said.

"We didn't miss anything. And I'm not taking one step back towards Mbanza."

Piper groaned with frustration. "Cammy, I need you to meet me halfway here. Your attitude isn't helping. I'm doing my best to come up with ideas here."

"I have an idea," Jody interrupted. He peered towards the town with a smug grin. "How about we get rescued?"

What are you talking about?" Piper asked. "Where are you going?"

"What did I tell you!" Jody said as he started to jog down the road. "What did I tell you!"

"What did you tell us?" Piper called after him. "What are you doing?"

"I told you the army would come!" he cried. "The cavalry has arrived! We're saved. I can see them now!"

"The army?" Piper squeaked. "They're here?" Piper looked down the road. "Oh, my god. I see them too. They're coming this way. Jody, you were right!"

Jody didn't respond. He was running at full speed, waiving his devil stick, and calling out into the darkness. While Piper bounced from side to side, unable to control her glee, Camden got gingerly to his feet. He squinted and saw a group of men marching up the road. Framed by the burning town, they were merely silhouettes, but they had the silhouettes of soldiers. They were carrying guns and wearing helmets. In Camden's limited experience, army soldiers, not rioting townspeople, wore helmets. But he had an uneasy feeling. As much as he liked the idea of being rescued, something didn't sit well. That was when he noticed the color of the helmets.

Having bounced herself silly, Piper took a step to start after Jody. Camden reached out and caught her by the arm.

Piper flashed his hand a nasty look. "What is it, Cammy?" she said. "What are you doing?"

"Just stop for a second," Camden growled. "Look at those helmets. Aren't those blue helmets?"

Piper obliged and took a look. "I guess so. Sure. What about it?" she asked impatiently.

"Remember the soldiers in the tent? They wore blue helmets too. Right before the mob got them.

Piper stopped bouncing. Her face went pale. "Maybe they're other soldiers that, you know, have the same helmets. Maybe that's just the uniform?"

"Maybe," Camden said. "But if the army is here to stop the riot, why are they coming towards us? Shouldn't they be going to the town?"

This question had not occurred to Piper. Nor had it occurred to Jody, who had just reached the men in the blue helmets. Piper and Camden watched from a distance as Jody paused, looked the new arrivals over, and then fled back up the road. The men in the blue helmets raced after him. The chase ended quickly when one of the men in the blue helmets lifted a rifle and fired. Jody screamed out and collapsed on the road, holding his leg. He only stopped screaming when the men in blue helmets swarmed around him.

Camden and Piper looked on in horror. After chasing Jody down, the blue helmets were close enough to be clearly seen. They were not army. They were villagers equipped with the plunder of the fallen peacekeepers.

Piper mumbled incoherently. Camden's shredded feet felt like lead weights sunk into the dirt. The mob was sure to see them any minute, but neither could move. Left to their own devices, they would have been goners. But, fortunately, there was an intervening force. Through his shock, Camden was vaguely aware of rustling grass behind him. A moment later, a hand covered his mouth, and he and Piper were pulled from the road. After he was dragged into the tall grass, Camden's survival instincts belatedly kicked in. As he was pushed onto his stomach, he twisted his head free from the hand that muzzled him. He turned towards his assailant. He might have screamed, but the sight of his attacker robbed him of words.

Hidden in the savanna grass, Camden found himself face-to-face with Olson. Or face-to-half-a-face anyway. Where Olson's cheek had once been, there was a ragged hole. Camden stared in shock. Olson stared back and raised a finger to his lips. Attempting to make a shooshing sound, a fine mist of blood sprayed from his cheek like water from a whale's blow hole.

17

"You're a lucky boy. It's good that I found you," Kruger boomed from the tank's driver seat. He had no choice but to shout. He was competing with a 580-horsepower engine and the constant plinking of rocks and bullets off the armor exterior. "If I hadn't almost run you over . . ." he started, but abruptly trailed off, craning his neck and twisting his head to see through the navigation periscope with his good, unpatched eye. As he looked through the periscope, he shifted uncomfortably in his seat.

Jammu sat in the back of the cabin, trying to keep his goat from sliding across the metal floor. Although he knew that Kruger could not see him, Jammu tried not to make eye contact with the eye patch peeking in his direction.

"Oh, it's too terrible. I don't even want to think about what might have happened," Kruger said, resuming his monologue. "If you were lucky, you'd be dead and your goat would be dinner in someone's belly. No one in Mbanza has seen meat in weeks and your little friend would make a nice kebab. And if you were unlucky, you would be a kebab too. Believe me, I've seen what hunger can make men do. It can drive them mad. You and your goat might have even roasted on the very same spit! But then again, they could have just as well eaten you raw. I once heard . . . "

Kruger continued to riff on the unfortunate ends that could have befallen Jammu. For someone who claimed to *not* want to think about such things, Kruger had a fertile imagination. Jammu sat in the far corner of the cabin, stroking his goat, and tried to ignore the Afrikaner. He preferred not to dwell on the gruesome turns his night could have taken, but it would be rude to interrupt the man who saved his life.

Kruger's morbid speculations only stopped when he needed to focus on turning the tank. Grimacing as he peered through the periscope, he cut the steering wheel hard. Twenty-five tons of steel can build considerable momentum, and the centrifugal force the turn generated threw Jammu to the floor and sent his goat skittering into a wall.

The maneuver complete and the tank on a straight course, Kruger started talking again. "I have only met you twice. And I've already saved your life twice. You have a special talent for finding trouble, don't you?"

"Unfortunately, that is true," Jammu said as he lifted himself off the floor. "I am only a young goatherd, but I have had so much trouble. In one week, I have been attacked, robbed, and beaten. I was lost on the savanna, and I starved in a city. Just tonight, I watched witches cast magic spells, and I was nearly killed by a mob. But of all these things, the worst by far is that I have lost my flock. And without my flock. . ."

"Yes, yes, yes," Kruger interrupted. "And without your flock, you have nothing to offer the woman that you love. Whatever her name is."

"Her name is Nana," Jammu said with reverence.

"I don't care what her name is. You told me this story already. I don't need to hear it again. But if it's any consolation, I agree that you have had a bad time. Does that make you feel better?"

"Not really," Jammu said.

"That's just part of growing up. At a certain point, nothing makes you feel better."

"But I'm only fifteen."

"Fifteen is old enough."

Kruger continued to shift in his seat. He rocked from side to side and opened and closed his patched pantlegs like a bird flapping a pair of quilted wings. Jammu had once seen a man sit on a hill of fire ants. That man moved like Kruger did now. Driven by his discomfort, Kruger removed his eye from the periscope and scratched at his crotch. This distraction only lasted a moment, but it was enough time for the tank to strike something large and inert.

Jammu was thrown forward again. The little goat, which had only just recovered from the last fall, shot across the cabin like an artillery shell. Kruger hit his head against the periscope and a flurry of Afrikaans curses sprang from his lips.

"How does anyone drive this thing? Who can see out of this damn periscope!" he growled.

Jammu thought that the obvious answer was "someone with two eyes," but he held his tongue. He didn't want to antagonize a large man in a confined space.

144

"Whoever designed this machine should be shot as a war criminal," Kruger continued. "It's inhuman. It's cruel to make someone sit in such a small space. This tank is made for pygmies, not men. And good god, they don't even have a toilet!" he fumed with particular vehemence. His turned and searched the cabin, desperately hoping that there might be a bathroom that he had missed. But, unfortunately, Kruger had missed nothing.

Still cursing, Kruger put the tank back into gear. He pressed his eye to the periscope and worried his lower lip, combing his soul patch with his teeth.

When Kruger had calmed down, Jammu dared to speak.

"Where are we going?" he asked.

"Anywhere but here," Kruger said. "There will be no more work for me in Mbanza. I doubt anyone is left alive to me miss me, the tank, or the shipment of weapons. We're going to go as far as we can. And the sooner the better."

"Better because we'll be safe?" Jammu asked.

"We're safe right now," Kruger said. "We're in a tank. It doesn't get any safer than that. No, the sooner we leave Mbanza, the sooner I can piss. Oh god, I need to piss," he said.

Kruger resumed squirming in the driver's seat, and the goat staggered back to Jammu. It was still wobbly from being launched across the cabin. Jammu guided it to a tarp that covered a crate of machine guns. Once the goat was bedded down, Jammu resumed the conversation.

"How far can we go in the tank?" he asked.

"Far enough," Kruger said. "We have a lot of gas. And it's a *light* tank, so it will get good gas mileage as far as tanks go. Once we clear out of Mbanza, we can go wherever we want. That is, if we ever get out of Mbanza," he said, his tone darkening. "How I am I supposed to see where I'm going when everything is on fire."

"Could we get to Unubi?" Jammu asked.

"Unubi? Why would we want to go there? Does it have an airport? Or a gas station?

"Unubi has none of these things," Jammu said. "But it does have Nana."

"Nana again?" Kruger grumbled. "I thought you already lost her forever?"

"Maybe there is still time," Jammu said. "She hasn't married Teacher Mapouro yet."

"But isn't Mapouro very rich, and you have nothing? I may have saved your life, but you're still as poor as dirt."

"It is true. I am a poor orphan without a herd. I do not have a penny to my name. But, perhaps, there are things that are better than goats. Better than even money." Jammu looked around the tank cabin. His eyes twinkled with possibility. "Perhaps a tank is such a thing. Even Teacher Mapouro does not have a tank. If I returned to Unubi in a machine like this, I would be someone. Her family will be unable to deny me if I have a tank."

"Don't get ahead of yourself, you cheeky shit," Kruger said. "This is my tank, not yours. And my tank is not going to Unubi."

"But with this tank, I could have Nana!" Jammu said.

"Forget the girl. You're young. You can find someone else in another village. The world is a big place. There are other fish in the sea."

"There are no fish like my Nana," Jammu insisted.

With Kruger distracted by the conversation, the cabin shook again as the tank collided with something in the burning town. Jammu fell forward. Kruger growled with fury and glared at the periscope as though he might tear it from its fixture. The Afrikaner suddenly spun around and turned his rage-filled eye on Jammu. He slipped off the driver seat and crouch-stomped towards the orphan sprawled on the floor.

Jammu trembled before Kruger's approach and wondered whether he might be safer outside with the mob. As Kruger reached out his large hand, Jammu cringed reflexively at the hairy knuckles coming his way. But Kruger wasn't trying

146

to hit Jammu. Instead, Kruger grabbed him by the arm, dragged him across the cabin, and placed him in the driver's seat.

"You drive," Kruger commanded.

"Drive?" Jammu stuttered, still shaking from the misunderstanding.

"Yes, drive," Kruger repeated. "I want to get out of this town before I piss my only pair of pants. I can see nothing out of that damn periscope with this damn patch. You have two eyes – use them! Besides, if you drive, maybe you'll shut up about that woman."

"Her name is Nana," Jammu remined him.

"I don't care what her name is," Kruger said and crouched towards a hatch in the ceiling.

Jammu slouched in his seat and looked hopelessly at the controls before him. "I do not know how to drive," he said. "I have never driven anything in my life."

"It's easy," Kruger said as fought with the lock on the hatch. "You press on that pedal on the floor to go forward. And you press that one to stop. See that wheel in front of you? You turn left to go left. You turn right to go right. Do you understand?"

"No," Jammu said.

"Of course you do," Kruger said. "Just grab the wheel."

Jammu reluctantly did as he was told. "What if I drive into something?" he asked.

"It's a tank. It's made to drive into things." Kruger grunted and threw open the hatch. "Just listen to me. I'll tell you exactly what to do."

With the hatch open, the cabin filled with the smell of burning. Despite the inferno raging in the town, Kruger climbed up through the hatch and stood with his torso exposed outside of the tank. Only his patched pants were visible on the ladder below.

"What are you doing?" Jammu shouted at the pants.

Kruger ducked his head back into the cabin. "I'm going to navigate," he said. "I'm going to get us out of Mbanza."

"Get back in the tank! It's not safe outside. You could be shot. You could be killed!"

"If I'm killed, the tank is yours," Kruger said. "Now grab that wheel and press the pedal on the floor that I showed you."

Jammu hesitated. He regarded the pedal below by his foot with fear like it was a poisonous snake.

"I said do it!" Kruger barked. His words echoed angrily through the cabin.

Kruger's command had its intended effect. Jammu jumped in the driver seat and slammed his good foot onto the pedal. Twenty-five tons of diesel-powered steel roared to life.

Kruger's head and torso disappeared outside the tank. Jammu could hear him shout with approval as the tank lurched forward.

Jammu was pleased too. In an instant, all his fear and uncertainty had vanished. He gripped the wheel tighter as the machine quaked beneath his fingertips.

18

Camden pressed himself to the ground. He tried to stay as flat and as motionless as possible. Through the weave of the savanna grass, he saw legs stalking the road in the faint light. If Camden judged those skinny legs by their circumference alone, they were not so intimidating. Based solely on the dirty feet and the cheap flips-flops, they were not the least threatening. Outside the specific context of a prison shower, there are few sounds less menacing than the clip-clop of plastic flip-flops. But the casual footwear was deceiving. Those skinny legs conveyed men armed with clubs, pointy sticks, machetes, and the odd machine gun. Camden had seen what these men could do. And he had a good idea about they would do to him if they found him hiding by the road.

Camden had not flinched since he had been pulled into the grass. He lay sandwiched between Piper and Olson. To his left, Piper's face still reflected the shock of Jody's death. Her trembling chin was puckered like a delicate prune. Her usually bright cheeks were pale and translucent. Even her freckles seemed drained of life. Camden could hardly bear to see her so hollowed. But he could not turn away either. As terrible as it was to look at Piper, it was even worse to look at Olson. The man may have saved Camden from the mob, but that did not change the fact that his face had a gaping wound that bore an unsettling resemblance to chipped beef.

For what seemed like an eternity, Camden watched the skinny legs patrol the road. He listened dumbly to their unintelligible conversations in French. In the distance, he heard machine gun fire, shouts, screams, and the occasional explosion. One such explosion occurred very close, shaking the ground and causing Piper to hiccup with fright. In response to her involuntary exclamation, one of the pairs of skinny legs in the road paused and pointed its dirty toes in Piper's direction. Camden dared not breathe. He was sure he was a dead man. But he was mistaken – after a few moments, the skinny legs moved on. Miraculously, the African didn't see them in the grass. Piper's leopard print pants possibly helped in that regard by providing some camouflage.

The road eventually cleared. The skinny legs disappeared. The conversations grew distant. As the mob dispersed, Camden was still too afraid to move. But it gradually dawned on him that he might not die that very minute. Piper had reached a similar conclusion. A little color returned to her cheeks as she slowly emerged from her fugue state of terror.

Piper worried her lower lip with her teeth. Her eyes darted frantically in her sockets like two bugs circling an electric light. "What about Jody?" she managed to whisper at last.

"What about him?" Camden whispered back. "He's dead."

"How do we know that, Cammy?" she asked.

"I'm pretty sure he's dead, Piper. You saw what I saw."

"We didn't see what happened. Not really. I mean, we saw the crowd surround him. We saw them stomp. We saw them swing their clubs and fire their guns. But he might be alive, right? He could just be hurt. He might need us!" she said, her voice growing louder and more unhinged with each hypothetical.

Camden was at a loss about how to respond. Regardless of his past feelings about Jody, he didn't want to be insensitive. This was especially the case if he might still have a chance with Piper – after an appropriate period of mourning passed, of course. On the other hand, Piper was getting hysterical. If she got too worked up, she might give away their hiding place. For better or worse, however, Camden didn't get a chance to respond. As he struggled to find the right words, Olson slapped him on the back of the neck. Camden spun his head around, which he immediately regretted as he came face to half-face with Olson.

Ignoring Camden's expression of revulsion, Olson raised his finger to his lips in a silent "shoosh." He pointed furiously towards the road. Camden followed the gesture's path to a dozen skinny legs that ran back into view and converged around a spot on the road. Camden saw one pair of legs bend at the knees. The African plucked something off the ground. Camden peered into the darkness. To his horror, he saw a bright red clown shoe dangling from the African's hand.

Chaos broke out. The mob started to dash back and forth like hounds that had picked up a scent. The Mbanzans were on their trail and started to sweep through the grass along the road. Camden quickly realized that they could not stay where they were. But Olson was already one step ahead. As soon as the clown shoe appeared, he had gotten onto his hands and knees and retreated to thicker grass. Camden and Piper followed his lead.

Camden's feet were already shredded by running in his clown shoes. But if running in oversized plastic loafers was bad, crawling through the savanna was not much better. The gravel, stones, and pumice rocks rubbed his hands and knees raw. The grass was stiff and sharp. As Camden tried to keep up with Olson, the grass that Olson flattened sprang up and struck Camden's face like a flurry of paper cuts. After a very short time, Camden started to wonder whether crawling through the savanna was worse than the mob. But a volley of machine gun fire behind him dispelled that silly notion.

"It's all so terrible," Piper muttered as she crawled beside Camden.

"I know. This grass is like a thousand little knives," Camden said.

"I'm not talking about the grass, Cammy" Piper hissed. "I'm talking about Jody. And the others. What happened to them is just so awful!"

"I know, Piper. It's terrible. But their suffering is over. Just try to remember that they're in a better place," he said with complete sincerity as a blade of grass stabbed him in the eye.

"We only wanted to help people," Piper said. "We wanted to bring joy. That's what we came to Africa. But instead of joy, only terrible things have happened. Our friends are gone. The town is on fire. There has been so much violence. And I can't help feeling that I'm somehow responsible for all of this."

If Camden was being honest, he would have agreed with her. Piper was a little more than responsible for their current predicament. He could trace a straight line of cause and effect that started with her desire to come to Africa and the present miserable moment. But Camden held his tongue. There was no point in making her feel worse.

"I don't know. Who can say?" he mealy-mouthed. "This isn't your fault. This place was broken before we got here."

His words provided little consolation. Piper's budding guilt was tenacious. "But if we hadn't come, there wouldn't have been a show," she said. "All those people wouldn't have been in that tent. Lukas wouldn't have been there. The twins wouldn't have been there. And neither would have Jody," she said with a sniffle. "Why did I want to come to Africa? Is this my fault? Am I the one that did this?

151

Oh, why did I start that crowdfunding campaign? Why did I have to raise so many donations?"

As Piper built the case against herself, she became increasingly agitated. Camden was afraid the mob would hear her.

"It's not your fault," he said, trying vainly to calm her down.

"But it is!" she snapped back. Tears welled in her eyes. "It was my idea. I raised the money. Without me, Jody and the others would still be alive. Why did I have to care so much? Why is my heart so big!"

"But you didn't raise the money," Camden blurted out. "You didn't raise a dime of it."

"What are you talking about?" Piper asked. "You saw all the contributions on the GoFundMe page. I mean, you created the page! You said yourself that people from across the country gave us money."

For months, Camden had concealed the fact that he had bankrolled the trip. This secret had gnawed at him. That Piper threw herself at Jody while remaining ignorant about his own sacrifice drove him mad. All this time, he had remained silent on principle. But as he crawled through razor grass, away from a homicidal mob, principles did not seem worth the effort.

Camden gave up the charade. "Piper, the GoFundMe contributions did not pay for the trip. I did. I donated the money."

"You donated the money?" she asked with disbelief. She stopped crawling and grabbed his arm.

"Yes, it all came from me," he said.

"There were ten thousand dollars in that account."

"I know. Tell me about. I put it there."

"But where did you get it from? I've known you for years. You're always broke. You're not, like, some secret millionaire, are you?" She paused and considered him in a new light. "Cammy, are you rich?"

"No, I'm not rich," he said. "But it was easy to get the money. I just took out more loans last semester."

Piper looked at him skeptically. "Why didn't you mention this before?" she asked, still uncertain whether he might in fact be a secret millionaire.

"I don't know," Camden stammered, overwhelmed by the act of honesty. "I guess, when I saw that no one was contributing to the campaign, I thought it might hurt your feelings. I knew this was important to you. I wanted to help. I guess I didn't tell you because I thought you might think it would be weird if I fronted all the money. But, you know, Piper, it isn't weird. I wanted to help you, so I did it. That's natural, right? To help people you like? People that you care about? People that you, well, sort of love?"

Piper did not expect such a confession given the circumstances. Her eyes went blank. Her face scrunched up with confusion. She looked down at the ground between her hands as though she were searching the dirt for answers. When she looked up again, there was a strange and slight smile on her face. She reached out and placed her hand on his.

"Oh, Cammy," she said. "I don't know . . . I don't. . . . I'm so glad you said that."

"You are?" he asked.

"Yes."

"I've wanted to tell you for so long," he said.

"Well, Cammy, you should have told me sooner."

Camden could not believe his ears. When he choked out the words, he would not have imagined in a million years that Piper would be so receptive. Despite his shredded feet and the mob on his heels, there was a spark in his heart that kindled a flame. A warm glow in his chest spread through his body. He looked longingly into Piper's eyes. He wondered whether the time might be right for a kiss. Since they could die any moment, he decided that it was. But as he puckered his lips and leaned in, Piper rebuffed him.

"Oh, no, Cammy," she said, shaking her ginger head. "No, no, no. I wasn't talking about the part where you told me that you love me. That's very, very sweet and all by the way. But no. I was talking about you paying for the trip. I wish you had told me *that* earlier. Don't you know what that means?"

Camden did not know what it meant. He was dumbfounded with rejection and still wore his pucker on his lips.

"It means that it's not my fault. I didn't do this. I didn't do any of it. I couldn't have. If it weren't for you, I wouldn't even be here."

"Come again?" Camden muttered.

"Sure, maybe coming to Africa was my idea. But I couldn't have done it without you. You paid for everything. This might have been my idea, but you made it happen. There is no way in the world that this is my fault. It can't be." She nodded confidently, convinced of her blamelessness. "Honestly, if you think about it, Cammy, if this trip is anyone's fault, it's yours. It's your money that made it all possible."

The entire trip, Camden had cursed Africa, Jody, and everything else under the rotten sub-Saharan sun. But he had not considered things from Piper's perspective before. Judging from the lump that formed in his throat, he knew there was truth to it. Piper had effectively removed the albatross from her neck and tightened it like a noose around his.

Camden wanted to follow up on the point, to somehow return a share of the psychic burden that Piper had shoveled onto his conscience. But Piper had already moved on, figuratively and literally. Her leopard print leggings disappeared along the matted grass path that Olson had blazed. Camden started to crawl after her. But in a very short distance, he slipped down a little slope and rolled into the open.

Camden scrambled to his feet and got his bearings. He was on a narrow game trail. The trail was not far from the road – he could clearly hear the Africans looking for them – but it was sunken and hidden from view. The trail led into the

154

savanna. He saw Olson's hunched silhouette run down the trail and disappear behind a bend. Piper was right behind him. Unburdened from any sense of guilt, she bounded in her leopard print leggings like a pixie cheetah.

Camden had no idea where they were going. He had no choice but to cradle the albatross hanging from his neck and follow.

19

Jammu took to tank driving like a duck to water. Notwithstanding some minor hiccups and major collisions with flaming structures, he handled the tank like a grizzled veteran. If someone had given him a uniform and a furry hat with a bright red star, he would have looked like the proper child soldier.

Jammu's deft handling of 25 tons of mobile armor would have been impressive for any 15-year-old. But it was especially striking for a teenager who had received no martial instruction from video games or action movies. Jammu hadn't even ridden in a car until a few days before. He couldn't have come to the task any colder. His prodigious development was owed in no small part to Kruger. Despite his rough exterior and gruff accent – which were, respectively, as prickly and thick as a thorny bush – Kruger was a big softie at heart. From his station at the roof hatch, the Afrikaner overflowed with unhinged enthusiasm. While Jammu manned the controls, Kruger provided navigation, instruction, and crude exhortations to not worry about running into (or through) any buildings, which were, as he put it, already "foked" anyway.

Yes, Jammu caused much destruction. But omelets are not made without breaking a few eggs. And vast stretches of Mbanza were as flat as an omelet when Jammu was through with them. But under Kruger's tutelage, Jammu learned quickly. In practically no time the goatherd was guiding the tank through the flaming husk of Mbanza, negotiating narrow streets, and playing chicken with rioters.

His progress warmed Kruger's heart. Although Jammu could not see it, the Afrikaner wore a rare smile. His soul patch quivered with feeling. He had never had a son. But if he'd had one, Kruger would have wanted him to drive a tank.

"That's the way!" Kruger hollered down the hatch. "Give it more gas. We're getting out of here! And you're going to be the one to do it! Never let them say you can't, you motherless bastard!"

"I will not. I will never let them," Jammu shouted back obligingly. As an orphan, he was not accustomed to such kind words. But he honestly did not understand all the fuss. What was the big deal about driving a tank? One stomped on a few pedals and turned a wheel. There were much harder things in the world. Compared to herding goats, driving a tank was child's play.

On the subject of herding, Jammu glanced over his shoulder to check on his goat. Armored death may have been at his fingertips, but Jammu was still a goatherd at heart. His highest calling was to his flock, even if that flock had been reduced to a herd of one. The little goat was snuggly bedded on a tarp covering some machine guns. It slept, snoring softly, oblivious to the firestorm raging through the streets outside. Jammu nodded approvingly and slammed his good foot on the accelerator. The tank roared like thunder.

For all of Jammu's mastery of the tank, he had still not managed to escape Mbanza. Slums are not easy to navigate at the best of times. But a burning slum was something else altogether. Being lost was not a big problem for Jammu: he and his goat were relatively comfortable in the cabin. Kruger was a different story however. Standing in the roof hatch, he inhaled clouds of black smoke. Stones and bullets landed around him, plinking dangerously close to the crates of ammunition strapped to the tank. But carcinogens and lethal projectiles were minor nuisances compared to Kruger's chlamydia, which had chosen that night, of all nights, to flare up. His crotch burned like a thousand suns. He desperately needed a bathroom, but there was no safe place to go in a burning town. Kruger's was a personalized hell that Dante could not have improved upon.

After what seemed like an eternity driving in circles and spinning their wheels – or, more accurately, dual continuous tracks – Kruger found the way out. From his vantage at the roof hatch, he saw the way out of town.

"Go right, go right!" Kruger shouted into the cabin. "Now straight! Keep going. We have it this time!"

"Are you sure?" Jammu called back. He looked through the periscope. All he could see was smoke and flames. "It all looks the same to me."

"Of course it looks the same to you," Kruger said. "Everything is on fire."

"Then how are you sure it's the right way?"

"Because I see a sign!" Kruger exclaimed.

Specifically, Kruger referred to the green neon marquee atop the Hotel Internationale. The still-electrified sign floated like a beacon of hope in the dark night. Kruger guided the tank towards the gleaming letters, which represented both a lodestar of salvation and, almost as importantly, the promise of a peaceful place where a bladder could be evacuated.

As the crow flies, the Hotel Internationale was no more than half a mile away. But a tank, notwithstanding its others qualities, was no bird. Just as they reached the edge of the slum, the road terminated in a wall of flaming debris. The tank came to a halt.

"Why are you stopping?" Kruger barked as he ducked his head into the cabin.

"Because the road is blocked," Jammu said. "Don't you see?"

"Who made you the navigator?" Kruger growled. "Keep on going!"

"But there is a fire in the road. We have to find another way!"

"Why should we find another way? We're in a tank," Kruger reminded him impatiently. "Tanks don't go around. They go through!"

"But the fire!"

"You and your fire," Kruger scoffed. "Fine, if you are too afraid to drive through it, we'll blast through it."

"Blast?" Jammu muttered. "How would we blast through it?"

"Did you forget that you're driving a tank? And that tanks have cannons?" Kruger gestured angrily towards the control console. "Do you see that stick by the wheel? The one beside the big red button? Grab it."

Jammu saw a black stick on a control pad with several lights and a large red button. He placed his hand on the stick.

"That's it. There you go," Kruger said. "You aim the tank's cannon with that stick. Now push the stick left."

Jammu did as he was told. The cabin shook as the gun turret on top of the tank rumbled leftwards.

"That's it," Kruger encouraged, peaking outside the hatch to spot the gun. "A little more. Now push the stick forward. Down a bit. . . And stop. Now push the red button!"

Jammu reached out his finger but paused. He regarded the button warily. He had never used a weapon in his life. He had never shot a slingshot, much less a tank gun. He was predictably gun shy.

While Jammu's hesitancy was understandable, neither Kruger nor his bladder had any time for sensitivities.

Kruger called back into the cabin. "I said press that button," he commanded, his fingers already plugging his ears. "If you don't, I'll throw you out of this tank and do it myself!"

Properly motivated, Jammu complied. He pressed the button. The cannon fired. The tank, bucking with the recoil, rocked backwards and slammed back to the ground. Jammu had been totally unprepared for the force of the cannon. Saucer-eyed and deaf as a post, Jammu was in shock. It was like someone had placed a church bell on his head and rung it for Sunday service. The droning in his ears blocked out thought as well as sound. When the mental static gradually cleared, he heard Kruger whooping from the hatch.

"You blew a hole right through it!" Kruger cried. "That's the way!"

Still hazy, Jammu looked through the periscope. The debris blocking the road was gone. The way out of Mbanza was clear. Jammu stomped on the gas and the tank rolled forward.

They travelled down the dirt road that cut through the savanna. Once they left Mbanza, the air cleared of smoke and fire. The sound of gunfire receded and disappeared beneath the rumble of the diesel engine. They were finally free! If Jammu had his druthers, he would have driven until dawn and placed as many miles between himself and the doomed town. But Kruger had other priorities competing with the need to flee. After they travelled only a short distance from the outskirts of Mbanza, the Afrikaner shouted down the hatch.

"Stop the tank!" he cried. "Stop this damn thing now!"

They had not even passed the Hotel Internationale yet, which sat on the little hill above them. Jammu reluctantly obeyed Kruger's order. Once he stopped the tank, he looked over and saw Kruger's feet disappear through the roof of the cabin. Jammu climbed out of his seat and limped to the hatch. He looked out just in time to see Kruger leap to the ground. Jammu watched Kruger run to the side of the road and drop his patched pants to his ankles.

"We must keep going," Jammu called after Kruger. "It is dangerous to be here. The town is still very close."

"Some things are worth the risk," Kruger strained out, his voice wavering between agony and ecstasy. "But cut the engine. We don't want to attract attention. This might take a while."

After some trial and error, Jammu switched off the engine and returned to the hatch. While Kruger went about his business, Jammu kept watch. A ribbon of dawn was visible on the horizon. The sun would soon rise. Jammu prayed that they would be gone by the time it did. He surveyed the shadows and strained his ears for any sign of danger. All he heard was the sound of distant gunfire, and Kruger swearing as he tried to muster a stream.

Drops of liquid began to trickle onto the road. The trickle became a deluge. Groaning with long-denied relief, Kruger's mind entered a philosophical place. "You are lucky, Jammu," he said as he peed, apropos of nothing.

"Yes, I am lucky to be alive," Jammu agreed, nervously scanning the savanna.

"Not only that. You are lucky to be young. It is good to be young. Even a young cripple. There is so much life ahead of you."

"I hope that is true," Jammu said. "But if we stay here much longer, I am afraid my life will not be long at all. Are you almost finished?"

"There are some things a man cannot rush. And this is one of them." Kruger said. "Listen my little friend: I will never be rushed again. Do you know why?"

"Oh, please just hurry," Jammu begged. "We must leave."

"Because of that tank," Kruger said. "And the guns in those crates. Those are my retirement, my nest egg. Do you know what a tank is worth in Africa?"

"I do not," Jammu muttered breathlessly. He thought he saw something in the road, approaching from Mbanza.

"Well, I don't know either," Kruger said. "But I'm going to find out. It must be worth some land. A place to settle down and start a farm. It must be worth enough to put my days as a mercenary behind me. To start a new life. To be able to afford nice things like a wife and a family and amoxycillin. Maybe even a new pair of pants. Perhaps . . ." Kruger abruptly cut off as his voice was replaced by a heavy flow of liquid splashing onto the dirt.

As Kruger moaned with soft pleasure, Jammu stared into the pre-dawn shadows. He was now certain. There was something in the road. He squinted at a dark mass and distinguished a dozen men coming their way.

"Kruger, Kruger," Jammu hissed.

Kruger did not hear, however, over the sound of his thunderous urination.

Distraught and trembling, Jammu cried out, "Kruger, men are coming!"

On the plus side, Jammu's exclamation got Kruger's attention. Less fortunately, the men approaching from Mbanza heard it too. If they had not seen the tank before, they saw it now. Their silhouettes raced up the road. Muzzle flashes were instantaneously followed by the sound of gunshots and bullets bouncing off the tank.

Kruger looked frantically over his shoulder. But caught midstream with his pants around his ankles, he was unable to run. As he waddled towards the tank, he stumbled and fell into the road.

Jammu watched in terror as men rapidly closed the distance. He looked down at Kruger, flailing in the dirt. There was no one else to save Jammu now. He had to do something.

Kruger was still struggling to pull up his pants when the tank engine roared to life. He barely had time to roll out of the way as the tank lurched forward and barreled towards the charging mob. At the sight of 25 tons of diesel-spewing steel, the attackers fired a few futile rounds from their guns and turned tail, retreating back towards Mbanza.

With the threat dispersed, the tank slammed the brakes, spun around, and came back up the road.

"That's the way!" Kruger cried, pulling up his pants as he leapt triumphantly in the air. "You showed them what you could do! You showed them all!"

This celebration ended, however, when the tank rolled past Kruger without stopping, leaving the Afrikaner in a cloud of black exhaust. Kruger quit jumping and stared sullenly as the tank disappeared around the little hill beyond the Hotel Internationale.

For a moment, disappointment flickered in his chest. But Kruger grimaced hard and pushed that emotion deep down into his gut. After all, generations of Krugers had been born to disappointment. He'd lived with it his whole life. And if nothing else, Kruger was a practical man. With an angry mob about, he didn't have time to feel. The important thing was to keep moving before any rioters found him again. He crouched down and left the road. As he disappeared into the savanna grass, Kruger consoled himself that he'd just have to wait a little bit longer for the farm. The amoxycillin. And the new pair of pants.

20

Olson stumbled down the narrow game trail that cut through the savanna. Crouching to stay hidden below the grass, he could only see a few feet in any direction. With one hand, he pushed aside sheaves of grass. With the other, he tried to plug the hole in his face.

Olson blindly forged ahead. He only stopped to occasionally glance back at the two clowns bringing up the rear. He cursed their ass-dragging. He had gone out of his way to save Piper and Camden – the least they could do was keep up. Frankly, the girl had no excuse. She should easily match the pace of a man who had been shot in the face. As for Camden, he didn't expect the shoeless wonder tiptoeing down the trail like a roach on a hotplate to set any land speed records. But Olson had no sympathy for someone who was asinine enough to tramp across the savanna in their bare feet. He didn't have the time – or, judging by his soaked shirt, the blood – to humor someone else's poor decisions.

For what seemed like hours, Olson had bushwhacked with only the slightest sense of direction. He wasn't sure about where he was headed, or how far he had gone. This navigational uncertainty was only dispelled when he happened to crane his neck upwards and see the neon green sign of the Hotel Internationale. It was glowing in the middle distance, plain as day.

Speaking of the day, dawn had broken. While Olson was going in circles on the game trail, night had ended. The stars had winked out. The black sky had lightened to the shade of eggplant. A pale orange globe just peeked over the horizon.

Olson scowled at the sun – or scowled as best as he could with a hole in his face. He had hoped to be far away from Mbanza once it got light. Judging by the crackle of gunfire coming from the town, the uprising showed no signs of stopping. Once the sun was in the sky and the cover of night was gone, Olson and his ass-dragging companions would be sitting ducks on the savanna. There would be no place to run. There would be no tree to hide behind. In that unhappy eventuality, things would only end in one of two ways. With no shelter and no water, they could curl up into pathetic little balls and die quiet, thirsty, sunburned deaths. Or, alternatively, the mob could find them, which could be fast a way to go, but Olson was not inclined to rely on the mercy of a mob for a speedy death. In any case, neither option was appealing.

Olson pushed these morbid possibilities from his head. He was not yet resigned to a miserable death on the savanna. He tried very hard not to dwell on the negative, which was no easy task considering that his jaw felt like he'd been sucker-punched with a garbage truck. Fighting through the pain that radiated from his broken face, he started to work his way towards the hotel. Mbanza may be a charred husk. But if anywhere was safe, the Hotel Internationale might just be that place. That the lights were still on was cause for some optimism. Olson knew that the hotel had armed guards with machine guns, which were a requisite amenity for any establishment catering to business travelers in that part of the world. The hotel was located on a rise and had good sight lines, so it could be defended by a reasonably small force. If he could just make it into the hotel, they might be safe after all. And, if nothing else, the hotel had a bar. Even with a hole in his face – or, rather, especially with a hole in his face – Olson could have used a drink.

But he was getting ahead of himself. Olson crouched at the intersection where the game trail rejoined the road. The Hotel Internationale sat about 200 yards further up the road, across open ground. The savanna grass was lower here. And while being situated on a hill might make the hotel defensible, it made anyone approaching it a lot more visible. Olson looked up and down the road. He didn't see anyone. He strained to listen. The only sound was distant gunfire. The coast seemed clear. But he couldn't be sure. The fact that he was starting to see double didn't help matters.

While Olson assessed possible threats, the others finally caught up. Piper was the first to arrive and plopped down beside him.

"So where are we going?" she asked. "Are we going to that hotel?"

Olson didn't respond. If there was any positive to being shot in the face, it was that he didn't have to answer stupid questions. But while he tried to ignore Piper, he was struck by a wave of dizziness. The ground wobbled beneath his feet. He held out his arms to keep from falling. As he removed his hand from his cheek, his palm and fingers came away with a tacky sensation as though he'd been holding a leaky bottle of maple syrup. His vision swam. His eyes reeled in his sockets like a drunk on pay day.

While Olson tried not to pass out, Camden joined the group, limping along his other side.

"What are we doing?" he asked, grimacing with each tender step. "Why have we stopped?"

"I don't know," Piper said. "He didn't say."

"I don't think he could say anything if he wanted," Camden said, cringing at Olson's gruesome profile.

"Do you think he's alright?" Piper asked.

"You mean besides the hole in his face? He's lost a lot of blood. His shirt is soaked," Camden said squeamishly. "Hey, mister. Are you alright?"

Olson didn't respond. He slumped backward onto his butt and dazed. Assuming that further communication attempts would be unproductive, Piper and Camden conferred between themselves.

"We're going to that hotel, right?" Piper asked. "Where else could we be going? There is nothing else out here."

"That makes sense to me," Camden said uncertainly.

"Do you think it's safe?" Piper asked.

"How would I know," Camden said. "It's got to be safer than where we came from, but that's not saying much." He looked warily up and down the road. "If we want to make a break for it, the coast seems clear. . . "

He broke off and pointed towards the hotel. "Wait, over there. Do you see that? I think I see people," he whispered.

Camden was not mistaken. He did see people. There was a group visible against the twilight horizon. It was too dark and too far to make out details. But someone was patrolling the grounds of the Hotel Internationale.

"Are they good guys, or bad guys?" Piper asked, squinting at the distant silhouettes.

"I don't know," Camden said. "How are you supposed to tell?"

"Are they the army? Have they come to rescue us?" Piper squeaked, getting ahead of herself.

"Maybe. I mean, they might, but . . ." Camden said. "Who can say? They just look like a blob."

"Well, does it look like a military blob?"

Camden and Piper continued in this vein, arguing past Olson who teetered on the edge of unconsciousness. While his heart struggled to pump his dwindling blood supply to his brain, he followed the conversation with diminishing patience. Olson had not tried to speak since he had been shot. Whether he could was a question as open as the hole in his face. But he could no longer bear their conversation in silence. He opened his mouth and his jaw moved with a nauseating pop of dislocated bone. His throat rattled like reanimated death as he purged the blood from his vocal chords. Careful to move his lips as little as possible, Olson looked like a ventriloquist from a vaudevillian nightmare as he spoke.

"I've an idea," he said. His voice was hoarse and hollow, but intelligible. "Maybe you should stand up and wave. If someone shoots you, we'll know it's not safe."

Piper and Camden stared at Olson with shock. It was as though they had seen a dearly departed rise from a casket and deliver the eulogy at their own funeral. In their defense, Olson was as pale as a corpse and could have used a mortician's make-over. His face was made for a closed casket.

"You can talk!" Piper exclaimed.

"Of course, I can talk," Olson said. "It just hurts like hell to do it."

"But your face?" Camden said. "There's a hole it. I mean, dude. You look terrible."

"I promise I feel worse," Olson said and hacked up some gore.

Camden and Piper watched uncomfortably while Olson wretched. When he recovered, Piper asked, "The plan is to go the hotel, right?" Piper asked. "What about those people over there? Do you think it's safe?"

Olson wiped his lips with the back of his hand. He tried, and failed, to focus on the hotel. He saw double. He perceived not one, but two hotels, woozily collapsing on each other before separating as though undergoing some fantastic process of architectural mitosis. He couldn't even see the men Piper referred to. But he knew he couldn't wait around. He was going to pass out any minute. Olson wasn't crazy about the idea of potentially walking into a firing squad, but he didn't have a lot of other options.

"What do we do?" Piper pressed.

"We need to get to that hotel," Olson said.

Piper looked troubled by the response. "But we don't know who those men are. Maybe we should just wait here for the army. Someone must be coming, right?"

"Sure, someone will come eventually," Olson said. "The army could get here in a week. Maybe less. With any luck, they might even arrive in time to find our bodies before the hyenas get to us. Or a lion finds us. Or a . . ."

Piper shook her ginger head in disbelief. "A whole week? The army has to come before that. Doesn't the government have a responsibility to protect its people?"

"You obviously don't know governments very well," Olson said. "Now listen to me, if we stay out here, we're definitely going to die. But if we try to get to that hotel, there is a possibility that we might not. I admit the odds aren't great. But those are our choices . . ."

Olson stopped abruptly before he could finish the sentence. There was a faint rumbling beneath his feet. Then a discernable tremor. He thought he heard something. And then he was sure he did.

Piper and Camden were still hanging on his unfinished sentence.

"Unless . . ." Camden prompted impatiently.

"Unless we have another option," Olson said with a jigsaw expression that was meant to be a smile. Without further explanation, he got to his feet. As soon as he was standing, the vertigo struck again. The world started to spin. The universe wobbled on its axis. Knowing that if he fell down now he'd never get up, Olson focused on keeping his balance and staggered into the road. He walked, not towards the Hotel Internationale, but back to Mbanza.

Olson heard Camden and Piper hiss frantically after him. He didn't have time to explain. The hotel was a longshot at best. He doubted whether he could even make it that far in his condition. If he was right about what was coming up the road, it was his last best chance.

When the tank crested over the rise in the road, piled high with crates of machine guns and belching black diesel, it was the most beautiful thing Olson had ever seen. As his heart thrilled at the sight, a sight that was almost too good to believe, he realized that he might be hallucinating. If drowning sailors saw mermaids and oases appeared to Arabs lost in the desert, why shouldn't a grievously wounded operative imagine the miraculous arrival of mobile armor? That was just a risk he'd have to take. He had stopped seeing double. The world was now in triplicate. All he could do was hope for the best. He only really believed that he wasn't imagining the whole thing when Camden and Piper started jumping and screaming because they saw the tank too.

As he waited for the tank to arrive, Olson noticed distant shouting behind him. And not-so-distant gunshots. Both the shouting and the gunfire came from the direction of the Hotel Internationale. Olson didn't bother taking cover. The only thing that mattered now was getting into that tank. If they made it into the tank, the mob couldn't touch them. And if they'd didn't, well, that wasn't worth dwelling on. Olson lifted his arms, which felt heavy like he was hoisting a pair of kettlebells and waved down the tank. He would not let Kruger miss him this time.

Olson felt confident as the tank rolled towards them. His confidence was not shaken when the tank showed no signs of slowing down. He didn't lose faith when the tank nearly ran him over, swerving at the last moment to detour through the grass, missing him by a few feet. Thought came slowly to a blood-deprived brain, but it only dawned on Olson that the tank might not stop when it pulled back onto the road and continued on at full speed.

Camden and Piper chased after the tank. Olson didn't have the heart though, or the hemoglobin. As the tank disappeared over a little hill, his kettlebell arms fell to his sides and dragged him down to his hands and knees.

Although Camden and Piper had disappeared over the little hill after the tank, they reappeared almost immediately. Some distance behind them, Olson saw a group of dark brown blurs in pursuit. Those blurs came from the hotel, and, judging from their yelling and the flashes of gunfire, they did not seem friendly. Those blurs did not see Olson yet – at the very least, they weren't shooting at him yet – but they would soon enough. Camden and Piper were leading them right to him.

Olson sighed. It looked like he was in for a miserable death on the savanna after all.

If he was to be torn apart by a mob, Olson preferred not to watch. He decided to spend his final moments watching the sun rise over the horizon and reflecting on mortality. This reflection on mortality primarily involved cursing Kruger. Granted, Kruger was a soldier of fortune, but Olson never expected him to be quite so mercenary. If nothing else, he hadn't thought that Kruger would leave him to die when he still owed the Afrikaner a paycheck. Considering the fate awaiting Olson, the thought of Kruger not getting paid was a small consolation. But in dark times, one had to cling to something.

Olson noticed voices beside him. Camden and Piper had reached him. He glanced at them in a desultory fashion, picking up a snatch of their conversation.

"If we have to die," he heard Camden say. "At least we'll die together."

Olson looked at Piper's face. Her expression suggested that there was little consolation in this arrangement. But, as he wrapped his arms around her, she surrendered to his embrace.

Olson looked up the road. Now he could clearly see the oncoming mob. They couldn't have been more than fifty yards away. Maybe forty. The had stopped shooting. They were saving their bullets and evidently planned to use their gun butts, clubs, machetes, and other sundry pointy sticks. In anticipation of being beaten to death, Olson bent forward and extended his neck. He hoped that if he made things easy for the mob, he might have a marginally quicker death. At this point, a swift beheading was his best bet.

But as he sat there, his neck stuck out like a Christmas goose, Olson saw something in the dawn sky. At first, he thought it was a bird. It was shaped like one. But it was too large. It was too fast. And it was certainly too metal.

Olson gazed blearily at the drone in the sky. It was flying straight towards him. He noticed the shouts and heavy footsteps of the mob bearing down. It was as if there was a race between the mob on foot and the drone in the sky, and Olson was the finish line. As he wondered who would reach him first, he saw something detach from the drone's belly. It was like a big metal bird had laid an egg mid-flight. Of course, Olson realized that it was not a falling egg. But he preferred to assess the situation through a poetic lens, as metaphor softened the reality of a bomb hurtling towards him.

Whether it was an act of self-sacrifice, or simply an opportunity to cop a final feel, Camden leapt onto Piper, knocking her to the ground and covering her with his body. Olson wasn't one for grand final gestures. He resolved to meet his end with quiet dignity and look his death in the eye. And he would have, too, if not for the loss of blood. As he watched the bomb fall, everything went white and he slumped into the dirt.

A moment later, the mob was upon him, winning the race by a nose.

A moment after that, the bomb arrived.

21

Clean sheets. A soft bed. Air conditioning. And one-use syringes. The comforts of relative civilization.

With the narcotic attention of a drug-addled infant, Olson watched the nurse's hands remove a disposable needle from its plastic sleeve. His eyes were like two glazed donuts as he fixated on her nimble fingers flicking through the pharmacy of bottles on the bedside table. Taking a small brown bottle in her hand, the nurse inserted the needle and plunged up some colorless liquid. When the syringe was full, she flicked the tube and ejected a squirt the liquid. Olson gazed hopefully at the syringe. A glob of happy spittle formed at the corner of his mouth.

Olson appreciated the little things these days. The nurse with the fast fingers. The scent of baby powder and iodine. The plastic crinkle of the urine guard under his sheets. But mostly, he appreciated the morphine. Since arriving in the hospital, Olson had given himself up completely to the capable hands of the medical staff and its liberal provision of prescription opiates. As the nurse inserted the needle into the catheter in his arm, Olson tried to read the label on the small brown bottle that she had returned to the bedside table. Reading was impossible though. If his eyes were any more dilated, his pupils would have gone into labor. He couldn't focus on a thing. He prayed that it was more morphine.

Olson wasn't sure how long he had been lying in this bed. It could have been days. It could have been weeks. Maybe it was months. He didn't know and had no reason to care. For the first time in years, he was content. More than that even – he was oblivious.

Despite this generally vacuous state of being, however, brief bouts of lucidity did occasionally punctuate the opiate bliss. These periods were mercifully short, but Olson had gleaned some facts about the situation during his intervals of semi-consciousness.

First, judging by the hospital's quality of medical care and round the clock electricity, he was nowhere near Mbanza.

Second, although Olson had not left his bed, he was not missing any limbs.

Third, he had a roommate. A private room would have been ideal, but if a roommate was unavoidable, Olson couldn't have asked for a better one. The roommate was in a bed across the room, wrapped in bandages from head to toe. With his arms and legs in traction, he resembled a kinky mummy in a sex sling. The roommate did not move. He did not talk. And the tube inserted into his urethra eliminated any unpleasant tinkling from a bed pan. Aside from the occasional soft moan, he was as unobtrusive as a potted plant. It had been some time before Olson realized that he was acquainted with his roommate, and that Camden was beneath the bandages.

Fourth, finally, and most importantly, Olson discovered a taste for morphine. He liked it a lot. Without any prejudice to Tipo Tipico, Mbanzan rum had nothing on prescription opiates. As the nurse plunged the syringe into the catheter, his body tingled with anticipation. He already imagined the gooey sensation that would emanate from the injection site, travel up his arm, and radiate like pure goodness from his chest. He could almost feel the morphine spreading over him like warm oil, marinating and infusing him. His throat salivated. His breath bated. And then . . . nothing. None of these craved sensations followed. With annoyance, he realized that there was no morphine in the syringe. The nurse had only given him a dose of antibiotics.

Cut with disappointment, Olson turned his head away and looked up at the ceiling fan. Since arriving in the hospital, watching the fan rotate had become his chief pastime. It was remarkable how many enjoyable hours one could have with a simple ceiling fan and a morphine drip. But as Olson tried, and failed, to follow the fan's whirling blades, he heard a voice. Distracted by the false promise of opiates, he had completely forgotten that he had a visitor.

Gary sat at the bedside. Unlike Olson, he was not a patient in the hospital. He was damnably healthy, as fresh-faced and rosy-cheeked as a Franz Hals painting. But his red face went beyond mere well-being. He blushed with sincerity. Gary was speaking from the bottom of his heart.

"I really can't say it enough, Olson," he stammered. "I feel terrible about dropping that bomb on you. I had no idea that you were down there. It all happened so fast. It was fog of war stuff, you know? I'll understand if you can't, but I hope you can find a way to forgive me."

During Gary's apology, Olson had returned to his game with the ceiling fan. As he tracked the whirling blades, his head made a nodding motion. It was an unintentional gesture, but Gary took it for forgiveness. His red cheeks bloomed with absolution.

"Thanks, Olson. That means so much to me. You've taken a weight off my chest." Gary grasped Olson's hand with fellow-feeling. The physical contact tore Olson's attention away from the ceiling fan. Gary's eyes looked wet. Olson hoped to God he wouldn't start crying.

Olson's prayers were answered. The moment passed without any waterworks. Gary continued.

"The doctors are all saying you're doing great. Especially considering that a bomb landed on you. If that mob hadn't been there to absorb most of the blast, you'd be a goner. Or worse."

Gary looked guiltily across the room. Olson followed his gaze to Camden. Olson noticed that his roommate had a visitor too. A female visitor. He had a hard time placing faces these days, but the red hair and leopard print tights were a giveaway.

"Poor bastard," Gary muttered. "That guy is going to have a long road to recovery. Third degree burns. Broken bones. He got the worst of the blast. That girl made it out fine though. Not a scratch on her. Some people have all the luck," he said philosophically and abruptly brightened as he changed the subject. "But that's not you, my friend. You're looking up. The doctor said you're going to be out of this bed in no time. They're even going to dial back the morphine soon."

The prospect of a reduction in his morphine supply shook Olson from his narcosis. His eyes became alert with worry. His lips parted slightly as if to protest.

Unaware of Olson's junky affections, Gary misread the reaction. "No, don't try to speak," he said. "It's not your fault. You did what you could for that boy. You did the best you could. Just relax. Breathe. Focus on yourself. Focus on getting better."

Gary moved in closer. He inspected Olson's face and smiled.

"You look pretty good," Gary said. "You're going to have one hell of a scar, but your face is finally coming back together. When I first saw you, sheesh, you weren't easy to look at. You looked like Two-Face or something. Your cheek was so infected that you developed a fistula. They talked about amputation, but how do you amputate a face? I thought you were a goner. But it's much better now. The skin is almost completely closed around the wound. There's hardly a hole. It's no bigger than a dime. That's progress!"

Gary shook his head with bemusement. "A fistula. What are the odds, right?"

Olson observed the irony by spitting on his chin.

173

"Well, I should let you get some more rest. I've been chewing your ear off long enough. But before I go." Gary produced an envelope and placed it on the bedside table. "It's a letter for you. From headquarters. I hate to spoil the surprise, but you're going home once you can travel. They're giving you a desk job. You're not a field agent anymore. You've had one Benghazi too many and, with that kisser, your days of working as a linguist are over. You're being transferred to open-source intelligence doing translation work. Media stuff. Foreign news, I'd guess. I foresee a lot of French news channels in your future. Anyway, it's all in the letter."

Gary stood up to go.

"Just to let you know, this is the last time I'll be stopping by. Since there isn't really a Mbanza anymore, I've been reassigned. I'm leaving in the morning. I'd tell you where, but I'd have to kill you if I did," he said with a wink. "Take care of yourself."

He took a step towards the door but stopped. He turned back to the bed.

"Oh, I almost forgot. Just one more thing. Headquarters wanted me to ask you about that, umm, tank," he said, lowering his voice so others couldn't hear. "And the guns? Any idea what happened to them? They're all gone. There was no trace of them after the army retook the city. They just vanished. It's not cutting-edge stuff or anything, but you know the drill. A tank and a couple dozen machine guns could do a lot of damage in that part of the world it they fell into the wrong hands. And it could be a pretty big embarrassment for the agency if anyone found out we were the ones who lost it."

Olson did not reply. He had nothing to say even if he could talk. He had no idea where the tank was. Apparently, Kruger had driven off into the sunrise after all. If he ever found Kruger, he'd kill him. But he knew he'd never see him again. Or the tank. Or the guns.

Olson did not try to explain this to Gary. He supposed he could have written it down, but the subject was too sore and the betrayal was too fresh. He decided to play up his stupor. He drooled aggressively to head off further inquiry.

The tactic worked. Offering a final goodbye, Gary left the hospital room to play Xbox and reign death from above in some other godforsaken place. As Olson watched him go, he realized that he'd become lucid. Disconcertingly so. His body started to ache. His skin began to itch. Worst of all, he could feel his face. Olson looked plaintively to the nurse by his bedside, who was still sorting through the bottles on the table.

In addition to his sense of touch, Olson's hearing returned too. What had been an ambient wah-wah now clarified into distinct words. He could hear Piper carrying on a one-sided conversation across the room with the mummy Camden.

"I'm leaving on a flight tomorrow," she said. "I hate to leave you, Cammy. But school starts next week. It's going to be so weird without you. And Jody. I'll miss you a lot. I guess I'll see you once your back, but I don't want to pressure you or anything. I'll just be sitting in class, learning about stupid stuff like Shakespeare, while you're doing really important things. Like learning to walk again. You should focus on that, Cammy. That's what's important. Walking, I mean. I'll be sure to write to you. But not too often. I don't want to distract you from your healing. And we can talk on the telephone too if you want – once they take those bandages off and you can talk again."

She smiled down on Camden and patted his bandaged head. "I'll never forget what you did for me, Cammy. The way you threw yourself on me and took the explosion. If you hadn't, I'd probably be stuck in this hospital with you. We might even be roommates. Wouldn't that have been something? Maybe they could have fed us with the same straw."

"Just focus on getting well, okay?" she continued. "I know once you're out of those bandages, you'll be better than ever. Right now, you're like a moth in a cocoon. But when you emerge from that body cast, you're going to be a beautiful

175

butterfly. I just know it. I can't wait to see you spread those wings, Cammy. Take care."

Piper stood up and pecked Camden on the head. After she left the room, a low, miserable moan rumbled from Camden's adhesive shell.

Olson briefly felt sorry for Camden. It wasn't much, but any pity was a serious exercise of sympathy for a man with a fistula in his face. But in any case, the pity didn't last long.

While he watched Piper's goodbye, the nurse had inserted another needle into Olson's catheter. He was unprepared when he felt the welcome warmth creep up his arm, past his shoulder, and explode in his chest. After the morphine rode his arteries to the far corners of his body, he couldn't be bothered with Camden or anything else.

Olson knew that one day he'd get out of the hospital. That he'd leave Africa. That he would go home. But before any of that, the only thing that mattered was to take a deep breath and dissolve into his sheets.

22

Nana had never looked so beautiful. That's what all the mothers said anyway. While Nana waited, wistful and silent, by the river, the elder women of the village, the lady auxiliary of Unubi, fawned over her. They caressed her arms, fiddled with her hair, and sang praises to her youth and the manifest fertility in her budding breasts. As if in one voice, the mothers cooed that a woman always looked most beautiful on her wedding day.

The attention embarrassed Nana. She didn't feel beautiful. Not even with the romantic setting. The bend in the river was lovely. The morning light was soft purple. The dewed grass twinkled like diamonds. Mists rose over the swollen brown water like the breath of nature itself. Nana was dressed in white – or as near as anything came to white in Unubi – wearing the wedding dress that only two sisters had been married in before her. Yet, despite all of these enchanting atmospherics, Nana felt ugly. She couldn't believe that others didn't see the ugliness inside her, that it didn't seep out her person and pores, spoiling the bloom of her proverbial lily.

The mothers told her that she should be proud of marrying the richest man in the village. But Nana didn't understand why marrying a man like Teacher Mapouro was a point of pride. Desperate for answers, she turned to her mother – her real mother – the kindly face among the women who crawled over her like flies on honey. But her mother had no answer to give. She only offered Nana a weak and long-suffering smile. Rather than expressing any hope for Nana's happiness, the smile implored her daughter's patience and resignation. For as surely as the morning sun rose, it was Nana's birthday. She was fifteen. And she was about to marry a man who was old enough to be her grandfather.

Nana looked past the mothers, down the red dirt road that led to the huddle of shacks that comprised Unubi. She could see the groom now. Teacher Mapouro stumbled out of the largest shack – the shack distinguished by the sole satellite dish in the village! – and started walking towards the river. Or, more accurately, he was carried towards the river. In anticipation of his wedding day, Teacher Mapouro had had a marathon drinking session and kept the village up until dawn. Together with a half-dozen relatives, joined less by blood than a desire to drink on a rich relative's dime, Teacher Mapouro had spent the last night of his advanced bachelorhood singing dirty songs and making increasingly inappropriate toasts about his bride-to-be. As a result, Nana had spent the last night of her maidenhood lying awake on her grass mat, hearing in gross detail how an old man planned to rob her of it.

The little village of Unubi was not far from where Nana waited by the river. The wedding party, which consisted of the priest, some village elders, and Teacher Mapouro (with, of course, two intoxicated kinsmen supporting him by either arm), had already covered half the distance. But Teacher Mapouro needed to rest. The wedding party stopped so that he and his kinsmen could split a bottle of beer.

Nana was thankful for any reprieve, even a short one. She knew in her heart that it was unnatural to marry an old drunk like Teacher Mapouro, no matter what the mothers told her. The mothers said that a husband's worth is not measured in good looks, strong backs, or full rows of white teeth. Good looks fade, strong backs bend, and teeth fall out – Teacher Mapouro was living proof of these truths. No, the mothers assured her, the measure of a husband was his wealth. And Teacher Mapouro was wealthy, the richest man in Unubi. He had chickens and goats. He had cows and cassava fields. "Just look at his satellite dish," the mothers said. "He has over 200 television channels! What lucky girl would not desire such a match?"

Nana could think of at least one.

To the hoots and cheers of his kinsmen, Teacher Mapouro finished the beer and smashed the bottle against a tree. The wedding party resumed its march. Nana filled with dread as she watched its approach. The urge to flee seized her. But the river blocked her on three sides. The only escape route was down the red dirt road, through the wedding party. She would never make it past them, and she was reluctant to even try, lest she give Teacher Mapouro the wrong impression that she was running into his arms to expedite their union. Nana cast about in desperation, but there was nowhere to run. She was fifteen. She had reached the age of consent. What choice did she have?

Surrendering to fate, Nana decided to spend the last moments of freedom before she was shackled by wifely duties in quiet reflection. She turned and looked out on the river. The pale sun reflected on the water. The birds sang in the sky. The monkeys shrieked in the trees. Nana wished she could scream too.

While Nana gazed out across the water, the wedding party arrived. The priest started the ceremony. Nana hardly noticed. His words seemed distant, as though spoken from across a great divide. She fixated on her husband-to-be. Teacher Mapouro was "standing" on the far side of the priest, still supported by his kinsmen. He hung between their shoulders like a scarecrow who had lost its stuffing.

Nana inspected his gray hair. His face's deeply plowed lines. His bleary, yellow eyes. His teeth were sporadic and crenelated like the battlements of a ruined castle. He did not only look old: he looked decayed. At first, the idea of marrying such a specimen alarmed her. But Nana was a smart girl and quickly saw the advantages of marrying an old man in ill-health. She was not even married yet, and she already looked fondly to widowhood.

When Nana finished studying the groom, she noticed that the priest was no longer speaking. The eyes of the crowd – the village elders, the mothers, her real mother, and Teacher Mapouro – were fixed upon her with anticipation. It occurred to Nana that they expected her to speak. It was time for her vows. Nana's skin turned to ice. Her mouth went dry. Blood pulsed in her ears. Reflexively, she looked towards the swollen river and wondered whether a watery death might not be a worse fate than marriage.

But as Nana grappled with this question, the silence was broken. There was a rumbling in the distance. From somewhere beyond the village came the sound of rolling thunder. The wedding party heard it too. The villagers looked up, expecting to see storm clouds in the sky. But the sky was clear to the horizon. Still the rumbling persisted and grew. The ground began to tremble.

Aside from Teacher Mapouro – apparently oblivious to the noise, his unwholesome smile fixed on Nana did not waver – the wedding procession saw 25 tons of mobile armor burst through the jungle and roar up the red dirt road towards Unubi. Stacked with weapon crates, the great metal machine exhaled black dragon smoke and shook the ground like an earthquake. The people of Unubi had never seen a tank before and watched with terror as it smashed through Teacher Mapouro's house, flattening his prized satellite dish, and continued on towards the river. Towards the wedding party.

The villagers fled in all directions, leaving the bride and the groom to face the tank. Teacher Mapouro, abandoned by his kinsmen and too drunk to stand, slumped to the ground. He teetered on his knees, staring blearily at the pile of debris that had been his home. Nana did not run either. She waited with her head held high, recognizing that one way or the other, the tank was her way out of a bad marriage.

The tank belched smoke as it tore up the road towards Nana. At the last moment, its dual treads locked. It skidded to a halt. Gears ground and steel scraped as its turret rotated and its cannon trained on Teacher Mapouro. The old drunk gazed into the 3-inch barrel leveled at his head.

After Teacher Mapouro was subdued, Nana heard a noise inside the tank. There was the metallic click of an unlocking door. On the top of the tank, a hatch flung open and a head popped out. Nana stared in confusion. It was the head of a small goat, which regarded the scene with mild curiosity and made goat noises. A moment later, a second head appeared alongside the goat. Nana could not believe her eyes. It was a familiar face. It was a face she thought she would never see again.

Jammu beamed down at Nana from the tank. And Nana beamed back. For the first time on her wedding day, she smiled.